The Treasure of Time

J.R. Ballow

Published by:
Southern Yellow Pine (SYP) Publishing
4351 Natural Bridge Rd.
Tallahassee, FL 32305

www.syppublishing.com

ISBN-10: 1940869455
ISBN-13: 978-1-940869-45-2
ISBN-13: ePub 978-1-940869-46-9
ISBN-13: Adobe eBook 978-1-940869-47-6
Library of Congress control Number: 2015943393

Author Photo: Brian D. Campbell ANC Photos Custom Photography Studio

Front Cover Design: James C Hamer
Front Cover
Copyright by JR Ballow

Printed in the United States of America
First Edition
June 2015

Dedication

I would like to dedicate this book to my lovely wife Lisa.

And to my late son Andy, who made me understand how important time really is.

Chapter One

Harry woke up as he did every morning, with the alarm blaring in his ear, a foul taste in his mouth, and the smell of freshly brewed coffee in the air. He slid out of bed and made his way across the marble floors of the penthouse apartment, past the collection of art few people ever got to see and into the kitchen. He poured himself a cup and settled down on the balcony to look at the newspaper that had been left at his front door, just as he did every morning. Sipping his coffee, he went directly to the stock page, looking for the miracle that would guarantee his more-than-comfortable retirement. Not finding it, he sighed and scanned the headlines to get the latest and greatest news in an attempt to stay ahead of his fellow mid-levels in water cooler gossip.

After having hot coffee and a cold breakfast, Harry made his way to the gym that waited for him at the end of the hall for an early morning workout. He found it relaxing to work out before heading in to the office in the morning. It seemed to get his blood pumping, and it cleared his head. He really didn't notice any difference in his physique from the routine, but only because he wasn't looking. Actually, the years of pumping iron and putting miles on the equipment had done wonders. He saw himself every day, and the benefits were so slow that they went unnoticed by Harry, who was always looking at the bottom line.

Harry was a driven man. He was always struggling to be better, constantly pushing the limits of his abilities by trying to reach the next level. He was relentlessly searching for the feeling of inner peace and security he'd never been able to find. He set goals, fought to meet them, and then, without missing a beat, set the next one. Harry believed it was the destination and not the journey that mattered, leaving him discontented upon achieving his goals. Harry was a handsome man and, although he didn't think so, quite a catch; he never felt he was good enough. Constantly trying to compensate for his unending feelings of emptiness with wealth and power, he never took time to stop and smell the roses. He was the type of man who went through his routine and reached for the next nearly unobtainable goal, without enjoying that party called life that everyone else seemed to have been invited to attend and enjoy. It was a lonely life that he, at forty, felt hadn't begun. Money and power were the focus of his existence, and enough was never enough.

Harry hadn't been blessed with rich parents who could provide him with a top-notch education. He'd attended a community college, working at night and on weekends to pay his way. He'd driven a substandard car and had lived in a substandard apartment. After graduation, he started working his ass off to get where he was today. Now, with a beautiful apartment, a fancy car, and a great career, he was caught in the trap of outdoing himself—a trap he didn't even know he was in.

The hard work not going unnoticed, he had been given a task that was sure to lead to that next tier. Recent economic changes had wrought havoc on corporate profits, and he was asked to come up with a business plan that would "turn things around." Harry worked on it for weeks, crunching numbers and doing research. It was a great opportunity for someone in his position, and he'd given it his best.

"Today is the day it will all happen for me." Harry was hopeful.

All the years of struggle and working like a dog had led to this event in his life, but he was feeling the weight of his efforts. Lately he'd been feeling run-down and found it harder to function. Working late into the night and through weekends, not taking vacations or holidays, seemed harder than it used to be. He blamed it on middle age. Although he sometimes found it difficult to concentrate, he pushed himself even harder.

When all this is over, I'll finally take a vacation, he thought, promising to finally treat himself. Or was he just kidding himself? After all, in the executive world, the others, "your friends," are always waiting for the chance to push you down and take your place. It really was a dog-eat-dog world; Harry knew it, and he wasn't about to let himself get eaten. Having pushed ahead of his peers by a slim margin, he now had a firm grip on the bottom rung of the next ladder and intended to retain it.

With the coffee gone, his morning workout behind him, and the minutes ticking away, it was time to get ready for work. After his shower, Harry stood in front of the mirror, buttoning his dress shirt over his large frame. He looked more like a football player than an executive. It was in his blood. He was a Kentucky hillbilly, only two generations off the farm, and at six foot two and two hundred fifty pounds, with broad shoulders and a narrow waist, he had to wear custom tailored suits; anything else looked ridiculous on him. He noticed a touch of grey starting to invade his wavy, brown hair and wondered how long it had been there. Dismissing the thought, he ran a comb through it, slipped on his shoes, grabbed his briefcase, and headed off to work.

Harry climbed into his Mercedes and drove away with time to spare. Stopping at a light, he noticed a dirty panhandler on the side of the road. The man appeared to be about the same age as Harry, but he looked much more weathered and was holding a sign that read, "Homeless, Please Help!" Harry couldn't help but ponder what had happened in this man's life that led him to this place, in this condition. He thought for a moment about the thin threads of life and how the small decisions that we make can grossly affect our course. He then took a five-dollar bill out of his wallet. He motioned to the man and stared into his face as he approached. The weathered man looked truly grateful, and he thanked Harry for his generosity. Then the light turned green, and traffic dictated that their time together was over. Harry felt he'd done a moral thing and had earned points with the Big Guy upstairs. Everything was a tradeoff with Harry. He felt that if he did a good deed, he earned points that went into a "good deed fund" from which he could draw someday. That wasn't the reason he gave the money; the man needed help, and five dollars was no hardship to him. But the points were a bonus.

Harry pulled into his private parking space, grabbed his briefcase and laptop, and headed for the elevators. Walking away from the car, he hit the button on the key and listened for the familiar chirping sound that told him the status symbol was safe. Entering the elevator, thinking about the meeting ahead, the meeting that would change his life, he was notably excited. The doors closed, and he was on his way to the office that had been his second home, and sometimes a prison, for so many years.

Unlocking the door to his office, placing the briefcase on the desk, the focused man sat down and gathered his thoughts. Turning around in the desk chair and looking out the window gave a marginal view of the city. Harry remembered when he was first awarded that office. The excitement of that day had since faded and become mundane. The thrill of the small office was now gone. In the eyes of many, he had arrived and should enjoy his life, but he felt that he was not quite there yet. He saw the achievements of others and wanted what they had. Not dating or going to parties; he didn't have time for hobbies or friends. He spent his time trying to get ahead, never stopping to figure out what he was getting ahead of, but trying just the same.

Chapter Two

The challenges were many for a mid-level executive in a major investment group. The name of the company and what they did was unimportant. The issue was that the company was in an uncontrollable financial tailspin. Profits were down and costs were up! Harry, gifted and dedicated, was working on a solution. If anyone could fix the problem, it was he.

His arrival at the boardroom a few minutes before the appointed time presented an unpleasant surprise. The meeting was not only already underway, but it seemed to be drawing to a close. There was an empty seat at the end of the table, opposite the chairman's seat. He walked to it quietly, set his briefcase on the desk, and plugged in his laptop, trying not to disturb anyone. The members of the board who noticed Harry looked at him with a blank stare, as if he were a waiter bringing coffee to the meeting, not the man with the solution to their problem. He tried to ignore them and set up his report. While loading the necessary programs on the laptop, Harry found himself fighting a twisting knot in the pit of his stomach. The feeling made him want to run out of the office screaming and hide under his desk. When everything was ready, he instinctively looked at Stan Jacobson, the CEO and chairman of the board, who was sitting quietly at the head of the table, listening to the presentation from one of the members. Harry hoped that his nervousness went unnoticed. He felt like a guppy in a pool of sharks.

Stan, relaxed in his seat and leaning on the left armrest with his hand supporting his chin, was listening intently to someone on Harry's left. When Harry looked at him, Stan glanced over, winked, and nodded, as if to say, "I see you're ready," then his full attention returned to the speaker, who soon finished. Stan stated, confidently, "OK, keep us informed and let us know if anything changes. I want to know before it sells!"

"Of course, sir. I'll stay on top of it," was the reply.

With that, Stan turned to Harry, who until that moment felt he was in the wrong place at the wrong time. Stan gestured toward him and said, "You all know Harry Stevenson. I've asked him to evaluate our situation and come up with an alternate strategy for us to consider. I think it's time we hear some new ideas from some new blood. Harry, the floor is yours."

Harry was impressed by that comment and realized that he now had the undivided attention of the entire board. He was momentarily fascinated by their total focus on a specific topic one second and their shift of focus to something completely different the next, with no time wasted.

"Ladies and gentlemen," Harry began. "My proposal may seem a bit unorthodox, but allow me to present it, and I'm sure you will find that it has merit."

Harry went into his well-thought-out plans to turn the company around. With charts and graphs, budget projections and business proposals, cutbacks and expansions, he laid out the company's future course. His audience listened intently, some nodding their heads, some tapping their pens on the table, but all of them giving Harry their undivided attention. His confidence increased as he spoke, and he made eye contact with each board member as he continued. As he panned his attention over Stan, he noticed the sly smile on Stan's face.

Finally, the presentation concluded. Harry opened the floor for questions. Through the questioning, Harry was able to sense which of the board members were open to new ideas and which members wanted to shut him down. Harry didn't let it rattle him. He addressed each one intelligently and completely, after which he thanked his audience for their attention and turned to face Stan, who was obviously impressed and summoned Harry to his office.

Arriving at the top floor, reserved for the executive vice presidents and the CEO, Harry made his way to Stan's office. He couldn't help but picture his name on one of the executive's doors. He began to fantasize how he would decorate the new office. Imagine having a personal secretary, a lavish office, and being the envy of all the underlings. That was power. That was what he needed.

Harry entered Stan's outer office and was greeted by Heather, Stan's secretary. Heather was a buxom blonde who looked as though she should be on the cover of a magazine. Given her appearance, she seemed to be a self-centered bimbo or a gold digger, but as soon as she spoke, it was apparent this wasn't the case. If she were a gold digger, or a bimbo who slept her way into this position, she was great at hiding it. She was a kind, considerate, married woman with two children, and contrary to popular belief, a pleasure to talk to.

"Hello, Mr. Stevenson," she said as she approached. "Mr. Jacobson is busy at the moment. I'll let him know you're here. Please have a seat."

"OK," Harry responded with a smile and took a seat in the outer office. He'd seen Heather in the building but until now had never talked to her. He figured, as did most of his peers, she was a snobbish bitch who thought she was too good for any of them. But here in this office, her demeanor proved this was not the case. And she knew his name. Impressive! She spoke to him as if they were old friends. He watched her figure through the tight skirt as she maneuvered her way back to her desk. One thing was for sure: if she wanted to sleep her way to the top, she definitely had the right equipment.

Anxious about the meeting and being called to the top floor, Harry stood up to take a look at the assortment of pictures that tastefully covered the walls of the outer office. They had one common theme. All of them seemed to be of Stan doing something other people only dreamed of. Stan on the company yacht *Dividends*, bill fishing in the Atlantic; Stan and friends dressed in climbing gear on a snow-covered mountain peak; Stan on a big game hunt in Kenya. Moments captured for posterity as an eternal reminder.

"How did he ever find time for all this?" Harry muttered to himself, and then, "It must be nice to be born rich." Harry felt sure that no one could do all this and work, too. It didn't seem fair.

A soft "ding" on Heather's phone broke the silence. She picked up the receiver, and after a brief conversation, said, "Mr. Stevenson, you can go in now."

Harry turned away from the pictures and headed toward the inner office door. "Thank you," he replied. As he walked past her desk, he noticed her family photos tastefully placed on her desk. One showed children opening Christmas presents; another was a family portrait with her, her two children, and her husband, a weathered, below-average looking fellow. How did he rate a looker like Heather? Harry wondered what she saw in the obvious blue-collar man. He looked like a gas station attendant. In fact, if Harry looked in the dictionary under "loser," he'd probably see his picture, but they were together, and the looks on their faces told a story of happiness.

"Unbelievable," Harry thought to himself, *"all this money and power around her every day, and she marries that guy? Go figure."*

Harry smiled politely as he walked past Heather and through the door and into the office of his dreams.

Stan walked up to him, presenting his hand, "How are you, Harry?"

Shaking hands, Harry replied, "Fine, Mr. Jacobson. How are you?" He remembered to grip Stan's hand with the proper pressure. "Don't break his hand, but don't hand him a limp fish," he schooled himself. He half-expected the boss to say, "Call me Stan," but that pleasantry was not forthcoming. Stan got right to the point.

"I've been watching you for quite a while now, Harry. We all have," Stan said, walking toward the bar in his office. Harry knew instantly that by "we," Stan meant the board. "Care for a drink?" Stan offered while pouring some scotch for himself.

"Scotch," Harry replied, walking slowly toward Stan.

By the time he got there, Stan was turning toward him with two partially filled glasses of the amber beverage. Offering one to Harry, he motioned to the leather office furniture that formed a comfortable living room in the massive office. "Have a seat."

Harry eased back into the cushy seat, careful not to spill his drink. "You wanted to see me, Mr. Jacobson?" he asked, trying to keep his voice even.

"Yes, Harry. As I said, we've been watching you for some time now." Stan explained, "We have an eye for upper-executive material, and you've popped up on our radar. We're looking for new ideas…new points of view, fresh eyes, so to speak."

"Here it comes," Harry thought, trying not to be too obvious.

"You need to understand that we don't make moves like this quickly, but we're considering you for an executive position. However, we don't know enough about you yet."

After a sip of scotch and a quiet sigh, Harry asked, "What would you like to know?"

"Well, Harry, you must know you were given this assignment for a reason, right?"

"Yes," Harry replied.

"You did very well," Stan said with a smile. "Did you think it odd that you were given a task as important as this?" Stan paused. "Think about it. We're talking about a proposed restructuring that will affect all of us. Didn't that seem a little unusual for a mid-level executive?" Stan waited for a response.

"I guess so, but I saw it as an opportunity," Harry responded.

"It was and, again, you did very well. But you were not the only one working on this problem. All of us came up with solutions similar to yours. We take the future of this company very seriously; our decisions will affect the lives of our stockholders, employees, and their families. Surely you didn't think it was all fun and games up here, right? We actually work for a living, too. It's a tough job, but it can be a rewarding one. Understand?"

"Of course, sir," Harry replied.

For the first time he saw the board in a different light. He wondered, *Did I think that?* He was focused on the goal, but did he realize there was work to do at this level?

"Look, Harry, all of us on the board are particular about who we bring into the ranks. Understand?"

"Yes, sir."

"Call me Stan in this office, Harry."

"OK, Stan." Finally, the gesture that set him at ease. "What do you want to know?"

Stan sat back in his chair. "Tell me about yourself."

"Well, I went to college in Florida, majoring in—"

"Wait, Harry. I don't want a résumé. Tell me about you."

"Well, I've worked here for—"

"No, Harry," Stan interrupted again. "You don't understand. The assignment that I gave you wasn't really an assignment; it was an audition. I wanted to see if you had the balls to operate at the executive level, if you could present unpopular ideas under pressure, respond to the opposition of those around you that want to see you—or at least your ideas—fail. People, who don't have the balls, cave in. You didn't. OK? Now, I want to know about you. How do you unwind, how do you live, what's your passion? Do you have a girlfriend? Do you like to fish, or to hunt, or to watch the sun set over the horizon? What makes you…well, you!"

Harry paused. He thought he was ready for anything that Stan would throw at him, but this was out of left field. What did this have to do with anything? How could there be any time for this nonsense in the executive world?

"Stan, this job is my life. I've been working on my career and future. I want to get my life on track before I take time to enjoy the fruits of my labor." Harry was sure this was the answer that Stan was looking for.

"OK, Harry, I understand," Stan said, setting down his drink on the coffee table. He had a noticeable look of disapproval on his face. "Look, life is too short to work all the time. You have to live it. Of course, you're expected to work hard, but that's only part of it. You're supposed to live the rest. If not, what's the point? You're what, forty years old now, right?"

"Yes, sir." Calling his boss "Stan" was forgotten in the moment.

"What are you waiting for? Life is short, and you have to enjoy it when you can. It's important to balance your life in work, play, and, of course, family. Material things can be replaced, but the treasure of time can't. Time is the most valuable treasure of all."

Harry sat quietly, listening to this high powered executive giving him advice that he never thought he would hear from a man in his position. How could Stan think this applied to him? Harry wasn't born with a silver spoon in his mouth. *Sure, it's easy to say this when you're born into money, but what about the rest of us? What was this arrogant prick thinking?*

"I never really thought about it, Stan. I guess I just enjoy working."

"OK, Harry," Stan said, standing up. The meeting was obviously drawing to a close. "You had your audition, and you passed it. Now I have another assignment for you, and this one is more important than the last."

Harry stood up and asked, "What is it?"

"I want you to find out who you are. Figure out what you want out of life. Only when you know what that is, will you be ready."

Harry was obviously puzzled and disappointed. Stan put his hand on his shoulder and escorted him to the office door.

"Harry, I expect the same great work you've been doing for us to continue." Noticing the disappointed look on Harry's face, Stan said, "Relax, Harry. This is the beginning of a journey, not the end. You'll find that more in life is about the journey and not the destination. And, of course, everything said in this office, stays in this office."

"Of course," Harry responded.

They reached the door, and then Stan turned to face Harry.

"I'm serious, Harry. You're being considered for an important position with this company. It's a matter that neither the board nor I take lightly, so don't you take it lightly, either. These things take time, and as I mentioned, this isn't something to be discussed at the water cooler. Loyalty and integrity are paramount. Being ninety-nine percent loyal is the same as being one hundred percent disloyal. Understand?"

Harry nodded, signifying that he understood, and the two men shook hands again. "Thank you for your time, Mr. Jacobson," he said with a smile, the formality indicating that he understood.

Stan smiled and opened the door. As Harry was on his way out, he heard Stan talking into a digital recorder about something different. He was again amazed by the way Stan could shift from one subject to the next. Not a minute ago, he had Stan's full attention; now Stan was deep into another topic, not struggling to get on track, but totally focused, just like in the meeting.

****

The rest of Harry's day was relatively uneventful. He was disappointed in the meeting with Stan and felt overwhelmed, because he wasn't in control of the situation. He realized that, up until then, he was a big fish in a medium-sized pond. This meeting showed Harry that there was more than fun and games at the top. Harry had always looked at the big bosses as figureheads—self-serving position-holders providing no purpose other than feeding off the efforts of the workers—oblivious to the real workings of the kingdom over which they presided. But now he saw there was much more to it than he thought. *These guys have a world all their own,* Harry thought, *a world in which they're involved in ways the rest of the employees never see.* And, for the first time, it seemed somewhat intimidating. He'd had a peek into that world and found that it would be challenging, if not a little bit scary. What if he wasn't good enough to be a part of it? He had a lot to think about and some real soul searching to do. "What the hell was the old man talking about?" he asked out loud as he drove home. What did any of this have to do with being a top executive? Was it a trick?

Chapter Three

That evening, Harry found himself restless. With Stan's words ringing in his ears, he couldn't just sit at home; he needed to get out. Before he knew it, he was out the front door and down the block, walking like a man on a mission. He didn't know where he was going, but he was getting there fast. He soon found himself at a nightclub several blocks down the street.

"The Boiling Point" was a nice upper-middle-class hangout he'd seen from his car but never ventured into. It was dimly lit, with smooth jazz playing in the background and comfortable seating. Everyone was sitting in little cliques, talking quietly among themselves. They were all trying to make themselves look better than they were and, most of all, better than the others in their clique.

Harry was surprised to see a few familiar faces from the office. Steve Simmons, Harry's one and only real friend from work, was sitting alone at a corner booth. Although they never did things together outside the office, they occasionally had lunch together and talked about whatever came to mind. Steve was the typical mid-level and the only one Harry trusted. Steve seemed happy where he was in life and didn't push as hard as Harry. He went to work, did his job, and tried to stay off the radar, biding his time until retirement. He wasn't interested in the race to the top. Harry knew this and found it endearing.

Steve liked Harry, too, and enjoyed hanging out during breaks at the office.

Harry walked over to the booth, and Steve motioned for him to have a seat.

"What's up, buddy?" Steve queried with genuine surprise. "I've never seen you here."

"My first time," Harry said as he slid into the oversized corner booth. "You?"

"No, I come here a lot," Steve replied. "It's a good place to relax."

"Looks like it. What are we drinkin'?" Harry asked, motioning to one of the pretty waitresses.

"Working class champagne?"

"Beer it is! This one's on me!" Harry said, handing the waitress a bill, adding, "Keep the change, shweeetheart!" in his best Humphrey Bogart.

The waitress smiled as she took Harry's money, stuffing it into an already overstuffed bra. She was on her way with a wink and a turn, leaving both of them staring at her best assets in a tight skirt.

"So what was up with the big bosses?" Steve asked, raising his glass.

The question snapped Harry back to reality. He wanted to talk about it in detail, but he remembered Stan Jacobson's words: "To be ninety-nine percent loyal is the same thing as being one hundred percent disloyal, understand?" He did understand that.

"Same old, same old," Harry replied. "A bunch of the big dogs just scratchin' fleas." And with that the subject was dropped.

Chapter Four

Harry spent the next couple of weeks working his project—trying to figure out just who he was. He watched TV. He walked through the park. He watched other people, trying to see who they were. He couldn't believe how hard it was. After all, he thought he knew who he was: a hard-working executive, upwardly mobile, and relatively successful. But was this all there was to him? He looked through old photo albums. There he was as a child, mowing lawns, painting the garage of his childhood home. Yeah, he remembered those days. He worked like a dog and saved his money. He'd come from a dirt-poor Kentucky family. He got a new pair of shoes at the start of each school year, and when they wore out, that was it—he went without. He remembered the summers in Louisville, barefoot and dirty, playing ball and riding an old hand-me-down bicycle.

Harry's father, Andy, was a bus driver. He was Harry's hero, a man's man, tough as nails, and afraid of nothing. He'd grown up in the Great Depression and worked on a tobacco farm as a boy. All sinew and grizzle, he stood six feet, two inches, weighed two hundred thirty pounds, and was handsome and chiseled with wavy dark hair and bluish grey eyes.

Harry always struggled to win his father's love and acceptance. Andy was up in years when Harry was born, forty-six to be exact. He was in his golden years when Harry was just a teenager. They went fishing together and played catch a few times but missed out on a typical father-son relationship. He loved the time he spent with his father, but Harry could tell that it was hard for his father to play the "Fatherly" role at his age. He was ready to settle down.

When Harry was eight years old, his father looked up from the morning paper and asked, "What do you want for Christmas?"

"I want a lawnmower, a gallon can of gasoline, and an extra quart of oil."

Andy looked at his son, confused. "What do you want that for?"

"I want to start a lawn business!" Harry said with excitement.

"Seriously, what do you want Santa to bring you?"

"That's what I want, Dad," Harry said as he left the room. His father went back to reading the morning paper.

****

And when Harry came down the stairs that Christmas morning, he scanned the presents around the tree, looking for the lawnmower. He didn't see it, but figured it must be somewhere.

Then he and his older brother Charlie began tearing into the packages and playing with the toys and games.

The magic of Christmas was like no other day of the year. It was filled with wonder and happiness, a day when both his mother and father dedicated all their attention to Charlie and Harry. They would sit quietly and watch as the boys opened the packages. They lived like paupers the whole year, but Christmas was different. His father made sure of it.

Andy told Harry a story once about the first Christmas after he and Harry's mom married. They watched the kids across the street play with an old tire in the front yard, the only gift the family's poverty-stricken father could afford. The kids rolled the tire up and down a hill, making the most of it. Andy told

Harry he vowed that would never be him. Harry knew his Dad saved to make sure there was always a nice Christmas for his family.

Getting to the end of his presents, Harry looked around, puzzled. *"Where's the lawnmower*?" he thought. It was what he really wanted.

His father, seeing him looking around, said "I heard a ruckus in the garage last night. I wonder if Santa left anything out there?"

Harry and Charlie went running out to the garage through the snow, still in their pajamas, the excitement of the day protecting them from the cold. When they arrived, they saw two, brand-new bicycles. Each bike had a bow on the seat and ribbons around the frame and handlebars.

Charlie ran up to the larger bike, smiling and laughing. "Cool…thanks!"

Harry was frozen in place, looking obviously disappointed. His mother and father looked first at him, then at each other, not understanding his lack of excitement.

"What's wrong, honey?" Harry's mother asked. "Don't you like the bike?"

Harry, trying to hide his disappointment, replied "It's great, Mom!" and turned to walk back to the house.

Harry's parents didn't understand. They turned to Charlie.

"What's wrong with Harry?" they asked.

"He wanted a lawnmower," Charlie replied.

"He told me that, but I didn't think he was serious. I figured he'd forget about it," Andy said.

The days after Christmas rolled by until March, and with it came Harry's birthday. He hadn't touched the bike; it sat in the garage, bow and ribbons still attached, collecting dust. Harry walked home from school and went straight to the kitchen where his mother was cooking dinner.

Pauline was a country woman who'd met Andy when she was just a teenager. She was a kind and gentle woman, and very pretty. Andy and her family were her whole life, and she loved them unconditionally. She was a marvelous cook and could stretch a grocery dollar far enough to feed an army. The familiar smell of her homemade chicken and dumplings filled the air.

"Hi, honey," she said as Harry entered the kitchen. "I made your favorite for your birthday—chicken and dumplings."

"It smells good, Mom," Harry replied.

"Dad has a surprise for you out back!"

Without a word, Harry went out the back door. There at the end of the sidewalk, in front of the garage, was a lawnmower, a gallon gas can, and his father placing a new quart of oil on the front of the mower. Andy then noticed Harry and pointed to the mower as if he were a game show host.

"There you go, sprout! Happy birthday!" Andy said, smiling.

Andy loved his son, and though he didn't understand it, the untouched bike in the garage told him how much the mower meant to Harry, so he'd put it together from spare parts in the garage and got it running. It wasn't easy making the mix-and-match parts work, and it was even harder hiding the project from Harry. But he did it.

"Oh, my gosh! Thanks, Dad!"

Harry was ecstatic. He wanted his own business, and now he was on the way.

Harry went to all his neighbors, offering to mow lawns. Before long he was working almost every day and all weekend. He watched his brother play with friends and saw games of stick-ball and hide and seek from behind the noise and vibration of his mower. His mother worried that he was missing out on life, but his father was proud of his tenacity. Harry worked like a grown man, reminding Andy of his younger life on the tobacco farm.

The lawn business was the beginning of an effort that never stopped, right through his teen years and into adulthood. The difference was that now, he was mowing through fields of paperwork instead of grass.

As a young man, Harry bounced from job to job, never spending more than six months to a year at any one of them. He grew bored and moved on. He traded his lawnmower for an apron and worked in a restaurant, from there a lawnmower mechanic, an auto mechanic, and then on to the next job. He'd master a job, learn all there was to learn, and move on, all while going to school. What did this say about him? Could all those years have really passed without his knowing who he was? It was as if he was so busy getting ready for life to begin that he missed the gunshot that started the race. It was like he'd gone to the movies but spent the day sitting in the lobby instead of watching the film. And there, looking at the photos, and remembering the boring journey that was his life, Harry had an epiphany. He'd figured it out.

"Oh, my God," Harry thought. "That's it! No wonder I can't figure out what my life's about. It hasn't begun!" During all the time Harry was trying to get ready for life, the best years had flown by.

"How could I have been so stupid?" Harry muttered. "I wasted all those years. No more!"

***

Harry went back to The Boiling Point with a different attitude. There was a smile on his face and confidence in his step. He'd already missed enough of his life; now he was going to live it. As soon as he cleared the door, he saw Steve sitting in the corner. He went over and slid into the booth while motioning to the waitress.

"What's happenin', bro?" Steve said with a smile.

"Everything." Harry replied. "Everything's happening."

"Whoa, dude, that sounds interesting. What's going on?"

"My life is going on, and now, I'm going to live it." Harry went on as the same shapely waitress from his last visit approached. "I'm done getting ready to live. I'm going to start living."

"What can I get for you, cutie?" the waitress asked.

"Jim Beam and Coke, and bring my friend a fresh one," Harry replied. "What's your name, hot stuff?"

She was used to guys trying to pick her up. It was an occupational hazard. "Who's your friend, Steve?" she asked as if Harry wasn't in the room.

"You remember Harry, don't you? He was here with me a few weeks ago," Steve said.

"Oh, yeah. I didn't recognize you," she said with a smile as she turned to get the drinks. "You look different."

"I am different," Harry replied, as she slid smoothly out of earshot.

"What's happened, man?" Steve asked, staring at Harry. "You are different."

"Steve, I just woke up. I've been living in the corner with the world passing me by. Those days are over." Harry took a deep breath. "I'm going to enjoy my life."

"No shit, Mister all-work-and-no-play, get-it-done-at-all-costs, damn-the-torpedoes, Harry Stevenson has decided to stop and smell the roses? What brought this on?"

"Steve, I took a long look at my life and realized that all I've been about is money and career. I never wondered why. Why are we here? What's it all about? What's the meaning of life?"

"Dude, you're going all Zen on me. You goin' through a midlife or something?" Steve asked, finishing his drink.

"What if I am? I've worked hard for it, I've earned it, and no one's going to cheat me out of it! I made a decision. It's time. I finally heard the starting pistol fire, and I'm off."

Harry motioned to the waitress, who was standing at the bar. "What's her story? She's hot!"

"Forget it man, she's outta your league," Steve said while chewing on ice from his drink. "Plus, she doesn't date customers from the club."

"Says you!" Harry replied. "Look at that ass."

"I know, I know. Can you believe she's single?"

"You're shittin' me."

The sound of the jazz in the background played on, but everything was going silent to Harry. Time slowed to a crawl. As the waitress turned away from the bar, her shoulder-length auburn hair flipped seductively, revealing her beautiful face. She was bringing their drinks, but all Harry wanted was her. As she approached, their eyes locked. Noticing his obvious stare, the waitress smiled back as she reached the table.

"Still waiting for your name," Harry said, not believing the words coming from his own lips.

"Beth," she said, in a smooth voice.

"What time do you get off tonight, Beth?"

"Easy, big boy. You just met me," she replied. "What makes you think I'd go out with you five minutes after we met?"

"How about the way that those beautiful eyes sparkle when you look at me?" Harry answered.

"Oooooh, a smooth-talker! Look, I think you're cute, but how do I know you're not crazy?"

"Who says I'm not crazy?" Harry responded. "Besides, Steve can vouch for me."

Harry and Beth turned to Steve who, until that moment, was mesmerized by the scenario unfolding in front of him. Realizing the two of them were staring at him, he spoke up.

"You kidding?" he said with levity, then taking a sip of his drink, added "I've never met this guy before."

Harry hoped Beth was feeling the same undeniable chemistry he was and that she would decide to take a chance.

"What do you have in mind, stranger?" Beth asked.

"I was thinking of the view of the water from my favorite restaurant. I like the way the lights from the buildings and along the shoreline reflect on the still water at night in such a way that it's impossible to tell where the buildings stop and the water starts. I was thinking how beautiful it looks."

"What?" Beth inquired. "I don't understand."

"I was thinking of how all of that would look as a backdrop with your beauty before it," Harry said slyly. "Have a late dinner with me tonight."

"Where have you been hiding this guy, Steve?" she asked, while looking at Harry and placing the drinks on the table. "He's quite the smooth talker."

Steve looked at Harry, who was oozing with self-confidence.

Before Steve could answer, Harry added, "You won't regret it."

"I have to be in my bed by midnight, or I get cranky," Beth said.

"In your bed?" Harry asked with a cool smile. "Or in a bed?"

"Well, I guess we'll find out." She turned away, then looking at Harry over her shoulder added, "I get off at about ten tonight."

Steve sat quietly looking at Harry. He couldn't believe his ears. He'd just achieved the impossible. Beth didn't date customers; she was untouchable.

"Who are you, and what have you done with Harry?" Steve asked.

"Steve," Harry said, sitting back and taking a sip of his drink, "life is short, and we ain't gettin' any younger."

"What other surprises do you have in that head of yours?" Steve asked.

"Well, you know, I've never taken a vacation," Harry continued. "I think I'm going to take one, a long one."

"Will wonders never cease? Where are you going?" Steve asked.

"I don't know. I've never thought about it before," Harry said.

Harry sat back and relaxed, listening to the music, waiting for the time to pass. He was looking forward to this night. The jazz played, the girls danced, the alcohol was served, and fun was had by all.

It seemed like only minutes passed, but it was already ten-fifteen p.m. Beth walked over to Harry and Steve with her purse and jacket and slid into the booth with them. She picked up the drink sitting in front of Harry and finished it off. She was a little nervous. Harry had been told Beth had a rule; she didn't date men she met in the club. She didn't think mixing business with pleasure was a good idea. He hoped she saw something different in him.

"We still on for tonight?" she asked Harry.

"You know it," Harry responded, staring into her deep green eyes. "Later, bro," Harry said to his envious friend.

Harry left the club with Beth clinging to his arm. They walked to the shiny black Mercedes, and with a push of a button, the lights flashed and the doors unlocked. He never thought of it as cool before, but Beth's reaction told him it was. They got in the car, and with the turn of a key and roar of the engine, they were on their way.

They headed along the freeway and down to the Hillsboro River, which was lined with restaurants and clubs that stayed open late into the night and were geared toward a well-to-do crowd. “That’s Amore” was one of Harry’s favorites.

The restaurant was authentic Italian by anyone’s standards. From the moment customers walked in the front door, they were immersed in Italian culture. The tables were carefully placed, each with a candle in a small, red glass that provided a romantic glow. The restaurant was divided into sections, each of which had a slightly different feel—ranging from the very traditional, to the more conservative, but all very Italian. The back of the restaurant was Harry’s favorite; it overlooked the west side of the river, and although there was no sunset at that time of night, the lights of the city reflected off the water, providing the romantic scene that Harry described to Beth back at the bar. The view was amazing.

As the hostess approached, Harry told her where he wanted to sit. She led the way, and Harry escorted Beth to the table. They sat together, facing each other across the small table. He’d never been here with anyone he wanted to be with. Occasionally, he came with a blind date some acquaintance set him up with, and although they were nice, and possibly even Harry’s type, Harry was never really into it. He thought the dates were more of an inconvenience, or even an intrusion on his time, than a favor. He felt his time was better spent on his career, or the acquisition of possessions and wealth.

But this time was different. He wanted to be here—with her. He wanted her. He was feeling a stirring inside him he hadn’t felt in a long time. He watched her as she looked at the menu. Her face was smooth and perfectly sculpted, like the face of an angel. Her lips were full and moist, her neck long and slender. *My God, she is beautiful,* he thought. He felt in complete control. So far, everything had gone smoothly, and with every move he made, his confidence grew.

Chapter Five

Beth was swept off her feet. Where had this guy been hiding? He was so full of life, so handsome, so confident, so mature, and obviously financially secure. *What's the catch?* she thought. He had a calm strength and a warm smile, was witty and handsome, strong yet gentle. He was nothing like the guys she knew. She wanted to learn more about him.

At twenty-two, Beth had dated quite a few guys her age, but she was always disappointed. She would fall for their boyish lines, rock-hard abs, and hot rod cars, only to be disappointed by their childish attitudes and lack of confidence. Not to mention that they were worthless. Long, loud evenings at sports bars and weekend benders at house parties were her usual dates with those losers. Someone would end up topless, others bottomless, and toward the end of the night, there was usually a fight that signaled it was time to go home. It wasn't what she wanted, but it was all she really knew. She wasn't looking for a sugar daddy; she just wanted to find a man she didn't have to support both financially and emotionally, someone reliable and emotionally stable, a mature man.

Since high school, when Beth's looks pulled her into the "in crowd," she just went with the flow. She was an intelligent woman raised with strong moral values. Her father, a strict, strong-willed man, kept her on the straight and narrow and made sure she was raised properly. She loved and respected her father, but his tight control didn't end when she came of age. She had become a respectful adult but could never do enough to please him. Finally, she moved some distance away to gain her freedom. She saw the strength of her father in Harry, mixed with the acceptance and respect her father lacked. This attracted her to him like no one else she had ever met. Harry was different. He was smooth and confident, and she felt fortunate to be with him. He hadn't made any sexist remarks, grabbed her ass, or even looked down her dress. He looked at her eyes instead of her chest, and he treated her like a lady. He listened when she talked and cared about what she had to say. He engaged in conversation with her, instead of "Uh-huhing" his way through the small talk. And then there was his physique. He was a large man with what she could only describe as "presence." He seemed to tower over everyone. She noticed other men stepping aside as he approached and women looking him up and down. He appeared oblivious to all this. She looked at him over the menu to find him staring at her with a pleasant smile. Realizing she had his full attention made her grin and blush a little.

"What?" she asked.

"I was just admiring your face...," Harry replied. "The detail of your lips and your eyes. You're a very beautiful woman."

"Thank you," she said softly, smiling at the compliment. "You're not so bad yourself."

"Would you like some wine?" he asked her.

"Sure, why not?" she replied.

Harry motioned to the waitress, and after getting her attention, tapped his finger on one of the wine glasses on the table in front of them.

The waitress brought over a carafe of the house wine and poured each one a glass.

"So, tell me about yourself," Harry inquired, setting down his menu and picking up his glass.

"What do you want to know?"

"Surprise me."

Beth thought for a minute, and then said, "I don't know what to say."

"What's your favorite color, your favorite food, your favorite sexual position?" he asked, smiling and without missing a beat.

The question caught her off guard, but she was surprised and a little excited by his forwardness. So far, he'd been the perfect gentleman, but she did like the glimpse of the bad boy that she met at the bar.

"Well," Beth paused and took a breath. "The color—depends. If it's a car, it's blue, if it's a rose, it's white, but if it's a dress," she said, motioning to the dress she was wearing, "a nice dress—low cut, short, skin-tight—it has to be black. I love all kinds of food; anything from hotdogs to lobster." And after a long pause, not to be outdone by Harry, and with a sly, somewhat coy look, she said "And as for my favorite sexual position…" She paused again, leaned forward, and said in a low, sexy voice, "I guess you'll have to guess by the sounds I make."

Harry blushed a little at that response while Beth watched. She suspected he had not thought she would answer that question, at least not this early in the relationship. She decided if he was stepping out on a limb, she could shake it a little. Shooting from the hip seemed to work for both of them here. Beth felt open and relaxed, and he appeared to be too. There was electricity in the air.

The conversation began to flow smoothly, and the sexual tension took a back seat to enjoying each other's company—a back seat, but still in the car. There would always be time for the sex, but at that moment, they were enjoying each other in a way that seemed so natural and effortless, it was uncanny. They spoke of old relationships, vacations, places they'd been, and places they wanted to see before they died. The conversation flowed, and the time passed quickly. At eleven forty-five, they both realized they'd barely touched their dinners.

"Quarter till midnight," Harry said. "If memory serves, you'll get cranky if you're not in bed by midnight."

"Well, technically, we're already in trouble," she replied. "I live at least twenty-five minutes away."

"Well…I'm only about five minutes away, much closer."

"Hmmm, that gives us enough time to get the leftovers in boxes," she said.

"Couple more to get to the car," he added, dropping a C-note on the table.

"We could just make it," she said. "Is your car fast?"

"Mercedes Benz. There is no substitute."

And with that they were both moving toward the door, completely disregarding their unfinished dinners. Their hunger was intense, but not for food. The sexual tension was back now and even stronger. There wasn't any wondering whether she wanted him or he wanted her. They wanted each other. The animal attraction was unmistakable. It came out of nowhere. She felt a little flushed and totally uninhibited. Harry could sense this, and it excited him. There was no planning—it was all instinct.

By the time they reached Harry's apartment, they were completely out of control. They were kissing and fondling each other as they got off the elevator that opened into his living room. Harry put his arms around her, picking her up, and she wrapped her long, beautiful legs around his waist, causing the tight skirt to ride up over her hips. Tongues explored the mouths passionately as they made their way to the bedroom.

She was his. He knew it, and she knew it. She felt herself surrendering to his passion and his experience. She would do anything he wanted. This was not a boy fumbling his way through his young manhood; this was a real man, one who knew how to take charge. He knew how to please a woman, and she was excited to surrender to his every wish. He had the strength of a real man, but with the respect and tenderness Beth longed for. He knew what he wanted, but cared about what she wanted, and he selflessly made her the focus of his attentions.

Harry laid her on the bed and hovered over her for a second, his mouth just a fraction of an inch from hers. As Beth leaned up to complete the kiss, he pulled back slightly, preventing the contact to heighten her lust. Then he climbed back and off the bed to undress.

Beth had never felt this way before. She stayed on the bed. That's where he put her, so that's where he wanted her, but she shrugged out of her dress, revealing some of Victoria's Secret's latest fashions. Beth wanted him so badly that by the time he came to her, she was almost in tears.

Harry climbed on top of her and began to enter her. He was careful and passionate, but she wanted him too badly. She put her hands around his waist and pulled him deep into her.

"Oh…my…God," she managed. Then she decided to let him take total control. Waves of submission flowed through her. She belonged to him, and that's just the way she wanted it. He was not like any other lover she'd known. Her body accepted the slow, deliberate strokes of her lover, and Beth found herself pulling him closer, her nails gently digging into his back. She could tell he was enjoying it as she slowly scratched his back.

He put his left hand under her firm ass and the other behind her back. It seemed he was pulling himself deeper with each stroke, and she began to climax, digging her nails more deeply into his skin as she cried out with pleasure. Instantly the selfless lover stopped and remained still during her orgasm, but as he felt her waves subside, he slowly began again.

"Oh, dear God, I can't believe it," she said, realizing that this was not the end.

She felt a rush of disappointment as he pulled out of her, only to become excited again as he rolled over on his back, pulling her on top of him. Still trembling from her climax, Beth instinctively slid down on him and began to ride. Her hands were on his chest, and his hands were around her waist, controlling her speed. She hoped the moment would never end.

It was at that moment that Beth realized she could never go back to the boys she'd known. Harry had ruined her for younger men. She was amazed by his patience and his control. He wasn't in a race to orgasm; he was taking her on a long journey, a journey of pleasure to destinations that she didn't know existed. This lover instinctively knew what she wanted and gave it to her. When she began to buck wildly on him, he gently pinched her erect nipples, slowing her down. When her arms began to tire, he pulled her down onto him and held her tightly. And as she had her second orgasm, he ran his hands down her back and gently squeezed her ass, heightening her pleasure. It was as if he were reading her mind, and through it all, Harry said nothing.

They were not starring in a pornographic movie. No one broke her concentration or interrupted her journey with talk. The body said it all, and by the time he'd reached his goal, she'd reached her third peak and was completely spent. She passed out on his chest, and Harry rolled her onto her side and cuddled up behind her, his strong arms holding her gently. The burning lust was replaced with a warm satisfaction. Their heavy breathing slowed as they recovered. And finally, they slept.

Chapter Six

Over the next few weeks, Harry began to learn a little about what it meant to live because of Beth. She'd lit a fire in him, and he was learning about life, day by day. He still had a long way to go, but he was making progress. He was working at his desk when he received an e-mail from Stan Jacobson's office. It, like most communication from Stan, was short and to the point.

Harry,
Please be in my office this afternoon at 2:00 p.m.
Stan Jacobson

Harry was in Heather's office by ten till two. Again he wandered about, looking at the pictures hanging on the walls, but this time, they seemed a little different. Harry had had a taste of the good life and wanted more.

He figured that Stan wanted to talk to him about the vacation request that he had put in. It was the first such request he'd ever made. Harry had been with the company for many years but had never taken a vacation. He had always been afraid someone would move in and take his position. But he was going this time, and it would be a long one. Harry was taking a month.

Heather answered a tone on her desk and turned her attention to Harry.

"You can go in now, Mr. Stevenson."

"Thank you, Heather."

****

Entering the room, Harry noticed Stan walking toward him with right hand extended. They shook hands, made their way into the office, and sat in the same places as the last time.

Stan leaned forward and picked up the two glasses of scotch he'd prepared just before Harry arrived. "Scotch?" Stan asked, holding one glass out to Harry.

"Yes," Harry said, smiling and taking the glass.

"How've you been?" Stan asked.

"Good."

"The reason I called you here was to talk to you about your proposal."

That was Stan, always focused, straight to the point.

"I want you to know we've decided on our new path forward, and some of your suggestions will be incorporated into the final plan."

"Thank you, Stan," Harry said with a hint of pride. "I'm happy I could help."

"Harry," Stan continued, "have you given any thought to the other thing we talked about?"

"As a matter of fact, I have," Harry admitted. "I've met a beautiful woman, and we've been dating. I've taken time to 'smell the roses' lately, but it's all new to me and a lot more complicated than I thought, so I've put in a request for a vacation."

"When was the last time you took a vacation?" Stan asked.

"I've never taken one."

"You mean since you've been with us?"

"No. I've never taken a vacation, ever."

"Oh, man, no wonder you've been having trouble," Stan said standing up. "Harry, you have to enjoy life a little. Come with me. I want to show you something."

Harry followed Stan into Heather's office.

"Heather, would you excuse us? Just give us fifteen minutes or so."

"Of course, Mr. Jacobson," Heather said.

She picked up her purse and headed out into the hallway, closing the door behind her.

Stan led Harry over to the first of the many pictures lining the walls. It was the picture of Stan on the back of the huge sport-fishing yacht *Dividends*, holding a huge kingfish. He was sunburned and his hair was windblown, but the smile on his face made it clear he was having the time of his life.

"This was two years ago, in the Bahamas." Stan said, pointing to the photo. "That king was fifty-two pounds, and I caught five more that day." Stan turned to Harry. "Have you ever been fishing for kings?"

"No, sir, I haven't." Harry replied, starring at the picture as if he'd never seen it before.

"You've got to try it some time," Stan said as he led Harry to another photo of himself kneeling next to a huge elk he'd just killed. He posed for the camera with his rifle in one hand and the other pulling up the elk's head by an antler. "This was four years ago in Wyoming," Stan said, triumphantly. "I tracked that elk for two days before I could get close enough to get a shot. There's nothing easy about hunting elk."

The next picture showed Stan on a snow-covered mountain.

"This is the upper portion of the Abruzzi Spur on K2. It's the second highest mountain on earth. Only Everest is higher. I thought I was going to freeze to death on that one," Stan said, shaking his head. "Glad I did it, but don't think I would do it again. Too damned cold."

Stan motioned around the office to at least eight other pictures as he asked Harry, "What activity is missing from this collection?"

Harry thought for a moment as he looked around.

"It's a trick question, Harry," Stan added, smiling.

Harry thought for a moment and then smiled. "I don't see any pictures of you at the office," Harry replied with confidence.

"Exactly!" Stan said with a reserved excitement. "Work is the necessary evil that gets you to the places you want to go."

They made their way back into Stan's office, and Stan closed the door. He motioned for Harry to return to his seat. Then Stan laid it out for Harry.

"Harry," he began. "We've decided to move ahead and promote you.... Congratulations. You're a hard-working man, and you've earned it."

"Thank you, sir," Harry replied enthusiastically.

"More than that, we need you. You think outside the box, and you aren't afraid of who you'll piss off in the process. I like that. And there were things you brought up in your proposal the rest of us didn't even think of. Well done."

Harry was smiling from ear to ear by this time. He was totally focused on Stan.

"Harry, we have big plans for you, and I need your head clear. It's good that you put in for that vacation. How long are you taking?"

"A month."

"Is that all you have after all these years?"

"No, sir. I have three," Harry said.

"Good. You need to take a vacation, but take all three months. Get away and collect some pictures for your own office walls. Take your girlfriend with you. Sow some wild oats; get things out of your system and feel free to use corporate resources. I want you relaxed and focused. You have a difficult road ahead. I must warn you that the rewards of the executive are great, but the pressures are equally great. You will be put to the test. Are you ready for that, Harry?"

"Yes, sir, I am," Harry replied.

"OK, then," Stan said, extending his hand to Harry. "Welcome aboard."

Harry took his hand in a firm grip. "Thank you, sir."

"It's settled then. Take three months off, and your office will be ready when you get back."

Stan escorted Harry to the door and held it open as he walked out.

"Enjoy yourself, Harry," Stan bid in farewell. "I'll see you when you get back."

****

Harry was on cloud nine all the way home. He called Beth and made reservations for dinner. This good news warranted a celebration. He wondered how this would play out. Things had been going well with Beth in the few weeks since their first date. He had his life; she had hers, and once in a while, they got together for their life together. It was a great relationship. She didn't crowd him, and he didn't crowd her. He loved being with her but really never looked past having a good time with her. They hadn't even spent a weekend together yet. Should he be so bold as to ask her to take this vacation with him? Would that be too much? Would he be crowding her? And more importantly, would they be able to stand each other for three months? What would happen to their budding relationship if he didn't ask her? What would happen if he did? He decided to play it by ear.

Harry picked Beth up at her modest apartment. She was wearing tight jeans with a maroon sweater that clung to her every curve and black, leather knee-high boots. Her wavy, auburn hair framed her perfect face as she approached the car and opened the door.

"So what's up, Harry?" Beth asked as she hopped in the passenger seat.

"Just happy to see you, hot stuff," Harry replied.

Harry pulled away from the curb and headed for the freeway. He didn't want to let on about the promotion or the vacation until he had decided whether or not he would ask her to join him. He knew she'd want to go, but she would probably have to quit her job to do so. He doubted she could get three months off. He also knew that if she quit her job to go with him, and she had a hard time finding a job when they got back, he'd feel obligated to take care of her. He wasn't sure that he was ready for that kind of commitment. He had been happy since they met, and they had an amazing sex life, but what did he really know about her? And what about the eighteen-year difference in their ages? Would she get tired of him? Would he get tired of her? Was he worrying too much?

Screw it! He wanted to take her with him. He wanted to make love to her on the company yacht, in the company condo, and maybe even on the plane.

"We need to talk," Harry said solemnly.

"What's wrong?" Beth asked.

"Can you get some time off?" he asked.

"I guess so," she said, noticeably relieved. "Why?"

"How much time?"

"A week or so, I guess. Do you want to go somewhere?"

"Can you get three months off?"

"I doubt it. What's going on?" she asked.

They were just pulling into the restaurant parking lot. Harry didn't answer right away, and she was becoming agitated. He was savoring the moment. He knew he'd be changing their relationship forever. "Did I mention that you look really nice?" he said, amused at how easily he could get her agitated.

Beth appeared nervous to Harry although he knew she was attempting to appear calm as they made their way through the restaurant.

The tormentor could see that his little game had run its course and said, "OK, let's get to our table and I'll tell you."

Harry smiled as he sat down. He picked up his menu and started to scan it, pretending to ignore her excitement.

"OK, we're here." she said, lowering the stress in her voice. "What's going on?"

"Not a big deal. I was wondering if you'd like to take a three-month vacation with me. Cruising around the Mediterranean on a yacht…, staying in a condo at Grand Cayman…, walking on the beach at sunset. But I guess if you can't get off work, I could send you postcards," Harry said, paying attention to the menu and sounding somewhat disinterested.

Harry looked up over the menu to see Beth's face light up with excitement.

"Oh, hell no!" she began. "I'll get the time off. Or I'll quit. You really want me to go with you?"

"Of course," Harry said, looking at her affectionately. "You do have a bikini, don't you?"

"Absolutely," she said, smiling and picking up her menu.

"How about a passport?"

"Of course. When do we leave?"

"I have a few things to finish up at work before I can leave. How about next Friday?"

"Fantastic, I'll talk to my boss."

Harry turned his attention back to the menu. "I think I'll have the steak."

****

Beth grew up in a small town. She was the only child in a poor house ruled by a loving, but overprotective father. He was quick to judge and slow to praise, thinking that a firm hand was the only way to raise a child, especially one as pretty as Beth. He was eager to keep her safe from harm. He was a decent man and would never have touched her inappropriately. Her father didn't realize that his overprotection was in itself harmful. She would have been damaged had it not been for her mother.

Her mother was a kind and gentle soul who spent her life making a home for her husband and daughter. She taught Sunday school and took Beth with her to make sure her young daughter was raised with proper moral values. She often ran interference for Beth, and it was the only way Beth got out of the house except to go to school or to the library. Her mother understood Beth's dilemma and, although she was worried about her daughter's virtue, put herself between Beth and her husband so her daughter could have some fun.

As a little girl, Beth had the same dreams that most young girls do. Being a fairy princess gave way to being a Girl Scout, then a cheerleader and developing an interest in boys. Finally not being able to afford college, she had gotten a job at a movie theater to work her way through. She watched as her friends came into the theater with their dates. She couldn't help but think there must be something better. She saved her money and, after she'd had enough of her father's control, moved away from everything she knew to make it on her own. She wanted to be independent and to earn her father's respect. And she was doing OK. She found a job in which her good looks helped her without compromising her integrity, rented her own apartment, and was doing what she set out to do. She was making it on her own.

Beth called home now and then, but the calls were all the same. First, she would talk to her father. The conversations would start out well but ended with him telling her what she was doing wrong and what she should be doing. Then she would find herself saying, "Can I talk to Mom for a minute?" The rest of the time was spent listening to her mom make excuses for her father and saying how much she was missed. By the end, she wished, more often than not, she'd never called in the first place. The phone calls became fewer and farther between, and then they stopped all together. And such was her life, until she met Harry.

Harry treated her with respect. After their first date, Beth knew her life would never be the same. That morning she woke up with him, watched him sleep for a while, and left while Harry was still asleep. Beth felt out of place in the penthouse apartment. She wrote him a note with her number, asked him to call her later, and caught a cab home. She had never met anyone like this knight in shining armor. Sure, he was wealthy, but that wasn't what mattered. He was a real man. A man with a strong will like her father, but with the ability that her father lacked, to let her be herself. He treated her like an independent woman, not a piece of property. He didn't just wait for his turn to talk, he listened to her. He was a giving lover, and he knew how to please her without worrying about himself. It wouldn't have mattered if he was a grease monkey who couldn't rub two quarters together; she would love him anyway. She didn't know where the journey would lead, but she was happy to be on it with him.

****

The next morning started much the same as always, with one exception. Harry was now counting down to vacation. He had a lot to do before he went, and he was making a mental list of errands he needed to tend to before it was time to leave.

Cruising to the office, he saw the same panhandler on the corner. His new sign read "Homeless Vet, Please Help, God Bless!" Harry stopped and signaled for him to come over. The man approached, looking relieved. Harry rolled down the window and handed the man a five dollar bill, which he took graciously and with thanks.

"What's your name, brother?" Harry asked.

"Holt," the man replied. "William Holt."

"Had anything to eat today, William?"

"Not yet," the tattered man replied.

Harry pulled another five dollar bill out of his wallet. "Get a hot meal," he said.

"God bless you, sir, God bless!" the man said.

Harry drove off with a smile. He pondered how a man could go from a soldier in uniform to a homeless panhandler. He wondered if he would ever pick himself up and make a life for himself. *Probably not,* Harry thought, *but at least today Mr. William Holt would eat.*

Harry arrived at work and began to make lists. Some were for projects that had to be done by others while he was gone, one for those that could wait until he returned but which he didn't want to forget, and a list to do before he left. He went about his business and ended the day feeling like he hadn't accomplished anything. He really needed this vacation. He was burned out, and some time off was just what the doctor ordered. He didn't even care if someone moved ahead of him while he was gone. It didn't seem to matter anymore. He had his promotion, the respect of his superiors, and he was getting the big office, the secretary, the power, and the pay.

Yes, the pay. He'd already amassed quite a nest egg, one large enough for most people to retire on comfortably. The stock market had been very kind to him as well, but it never seemed to be enough. Well, now it would grow even faster. His promotion had a lot of perks: better benefits, a company car, and higher pay. Maybe this time he was right. Maybe this time he had arrived. Maybe there would be time to stop and smell the roses, or the coffee, or whatever. Maybe.

Leaving the parking garage, he called Beth to see if she was ready to go. Harry went up to her apartment. She met him at the door with her luggage, and they made a final walkthrough, making sure that everything was off and secured. Then they left.

It was one less thing to worry about for three months. Beth would stay with Harry until time to leave on their journey.

Heading home, Beth told Harry she'd taken a leave of absence from her job at The Boiling Point.

"You quit?" Harry asked.

"No, just a leave of absence," she said.

"You think you'll be able to get the job back when we get home?"

"Who cares?" she said offhandedly. "It's just a job. I can easily get another one."

Harry had never looked at a job that way. To lose the security of a job without having another was unheard of in his world. He always covered his bases and made sure his income was secure. He marveled at the way she dismissed the loss of her ability to make the rent, pay the bills, or even buy food. He was sure she didn't have a lot of savings, even though she made good money at the club. She liked to shop. She loved nice clothes and shoes. She had a carefree lifestyle. It was one of the things that Harry really loved about Beth. She didn't worry all the time; she was totally at peace with herself. "Lose a job, no problem. Just go get another one." Simple as that!

****

Beth noticed Harry was looking tired. She wasn't concerned about the age difference between them. She just saw him as sexy and confident. There was a powerful, natural attraction between them that went beyond age. He wasn't focused on proving what a winner he was, because he was a winner, and there was the sex, of course, the amazing sex. But today it seemed as though the workload had taken a toll on him. He was a little less talkative and moving a little more slowly. Not a lot, but enough for her to notice.

"You OK, baby?" she asked.

"Of course..., why?" Harry responded.

"You look a little run down."

"I'm OK. I just really need this vacation. I didn't know how much until now," Harry added. "We'll be out of here soon, and I can recharge."

They arrived at Harry's apartment and decided to eat in and get rid of the perishables in the refrigerator. Harry was a good cook. Being a bachelor saw to that. He made dinner, and they sat down to enjoy it together.

"So, fill me in on our 'vaca'," Beth said, picking up her wineglass. She was trying to hide her excitement.

"Don't you like surprises?" Harry asked.

"I guess so," she replied. "Can't you give me a hint?"

Harry smiled. "Just go with the flow, baby."

Beth sighed. "Ooookay..., I guess I'm in your hands."

"Not yet, but the night is young," Harry said.

"Ooh, that sounds ominous," Beth said coyly.

They smiled at each other and ate dinner.

The day wound down with Beth and Harry on the west balcony of Harry's penthouse. The everyday sunset over the Gulf of Mexico took on new life. It was putting on a show just for the two of them, powering the mood of the evening, and bathing them in romance.

****

Strange that Harry had never noticed the sunset from the balcony before. He'd bought the Tampa penthouse apartment because it was the best. It had the most space, the best view, and the elevator opened into the living room. It was a sign of success, the thing Harry wanted most. But now he appreciated the apartment for different reasons. And at this moment, the reason consisted of the amazing sunset casting its light on this beautiful young woman as she stood on the balcony, sipping from her wine glass. She leaned against the railing, staring at the fading light of the day, a gentle wind softly moving her hair and the glow of the setting sun illuminating her elegant features. He gazed at her as she watched the last moments of the day disappear into the Gulf of Mexico. Her face changed color, as the sun changed from yellow to maroon. For Harry, time seemed to stand still. He walked quietly up behind Beth, put his arm around her, and pulled her back into his chest. She put her arm on his and nuzzled up to him. And as the night began, they enjoyed the last of the fading light together.

Chapter Seven

The next day was the last day at work before beginning the unprecedented vacation. Harry was ready, but he had a few loose ends to take care of before leaving. And something kept popping into his head. William Holt. Why was he thinking about him? He was a homeless man. Why would he give him a second thought? Tomorrow, he would find out. He was going to look for him on his way to work and talk to him. He was going to put it to rest.

The next morning, Harry slid quietly out of bed, careful not to wake Beth. He went through his morning routine and was about to leave when Beth emerged from the bedroom in one of Harry's shirts, sleep still in her eyes. Harry put his arm around her and gently pulled her toward him. She stood on her toes to give him a kiss.

"I won't be too long today. I just have a few things to attend to," Harry said softly. "I left you a key to the elevator on the table."

She looked into his eyes. "Am I moving in?"

Harry hadn't thought about that. He just wanted to make sure that she didn't get locked out of the apartment, but how could he tell her that? It was obviously on her mind.

"Let's take one thing at a time," Harry said. "Feel free to use the pool. I'll see you this afternoon." Harry thought he was falling in love with her, but he wasn't ready for her to move in. He wanted to see how they did on vacation first. He thought he'd handled it well. At least she didn't seem too disappointed.

But his attention now shifted to someone else—Mr. Holt. And he knew where to find the man. He didn't know why it was so important to him, but it was. It was like another loose end he wanted to tie up.

Harry arrived at the intersection where he usually saw the panhandler and parked his car. He saw the man across the street, and it was like seeing an old friend. What was he going to ask him? Was it any of his business? It wasn't, but what could it hurt? He locked the car and crossed the street. The tattered man saw Harry as he approached.

****

William recognized the generous man walking toward him, but wondered why he wasn't in his shiny car. It was obvious he was heading straight toward him, but why? Had he done something wrong? He felt uneasy as Harry approached. He didn't want any added stress in his life, but the man obviously wanted something.

"Have you eaten yet, William?" Harry inquired.

"Not yet," he replied.

Harry motioned to the coffee shop down the block. "Let me buy you breakfast."

"I don't want any trouble, mister."

"Call me Harry," he said, with his hand extended.

"Bill," the man said, as he hesitantly took the offered hand.

It had been a long time since anyone had shown him respect. He was usually looked on as subhuman, a lowlife. He was used to it. People stopped and gave him change, but they did so out of pity. Most didn't want to acknowledge he was a human being and didn't want to know him. It was apparent in their faces, and he didn't care. It was preferable that way. As he approached cars to accept donations, the disgust in their expression said it all. They wanted him to take the change and go away quickly. The car windows opened just enough to pass the money, then hastily shut, as if they were hand-feeding a bear at a dumpsite. He was alone in the world, and he liked it that way. No worries, no responsibilities, no one counting on him. All he had to do was stand on a corner and hold up his sign, but this guy was breaking the rules. Bill prayed he wasn't a Bible-thumper wanting to lead him to Jesus.

"What do you want, Harry?" Bill asked.

"I just want to talk. How about breakfast?"

"The mornings are most important. That's when I get the most."

"How much?" Harry asked.

"About twenty dollars or so. Enough to get through the day."

"I'll double that, plus breakfast," Harry offered.

Bill looked at Harry for a minute as if looking for the catch, but figured he had nothing to lose and said, "Lead the way."

They walked down the block together. Upon reaching the coffee shop, Harry opened the door for Bill. Bill looked at him for a second and then went through the door.

Bill noticed the other patrons in the coffee shop look at him, and then at Harry. He could feel their stares as he walked past them. It was something that he was used to. But he wondered if someone like Harry had ever had to endure such unpleasantness. Bill walked slowly toward a table by the window with Harry close behind. The dull drone of conversation was silenced in the circle immediately around them as they passed. The self-centered individuals leaned away and stared as Bill passed through their sacred space.

None of this affected Bill, though. He was used to it. It's hard for someone to push you down when you're already on the bottom. He reached the table and sat down quietly. Bill still wasn't sure what Harry wanted. But he was hungry, and this was a change from standing on the street waiting for handouts.

"What would you like?" Harry asked.

"Coffee and doughnuts," Bill replied.

Harry went to the counter and ordered a variety of doughnuts and two large coffees. Coming back to the table, he set the food down and slid into his seat.

Bill looked at Harry while opening the box of doughnuts.

Harry nodded and said, "Help yourself."

Bill was hungry, but he tried to maintain his composure as he took the doughnut nearest to him and bit into it. He closed his eyes and savored the sweet taste. It had been a long time since he'd had a fresh jelly doughnut. The ones he usually ate were a few days old, the ones nobody else wanted. Finishing the pastry, he washed it down with a sip of the hot, fresh coffee and looked at Harry. "Aren't you going to have one?"

"Go ahead. They're all yours," Harry said, motioning to the box.

"Thank you, Harry," Bill said. "What can I do for you?"

"I want to know what happened to you," Harry said, then seeing Bill's look of annoyance, added, "I mean no offense."

"It's a long story…." Bill said, trailing off. He thought about it for a moment as he began reliving the unpleasant memory that was his life. How unfair was it for this well-dressed man to dredge up the pain for his own simple amusement? Why would he even care? "What difference does it make? This is my life."

"I don't know, Bill, but I see you on the corner with that sign, and for some reason I just have to know," Harry said politely. "I've feared ending up in the same predicament, and I wondered how it happened to a veteran."

Bill looked at him, irritated, and took a sip of coffee. "What does it matter to you? You get off on other people's misery?" His hands began to tremble as the painful past flooded back to the surface. "You writin' a book?"

"Please, Bill," Harry persisted. "I mean you no harm. If it's too much to ask, I'll go."

Bill started to tell him to get out of his face. Or maybe bust him in the mouth for good measure, but he really needed the money, and he was still eating the doughnuts. He took a deep breath, looked Harry in the eye and made a decision. It didn't matter anyway now. Once his mind headed down that road, there was no stopping the journey. He took another sip of coffee and reluctantly started to tell the story.

"I wasn't always a bum. I was a man once. It started right after high school, I knew I wanted to join the Marines. And a week after graduation, I signed up."

Over the next hour, William Holt told a story that had Harry glued to every word. It was a life of misery and misfortune, spanning several continents and numerous battles that never made the newspapers. The last battle was against the family he'd spent the most time with, the Marine Corps itself. It was a battle in which he was framed for a crime he didn't commit.

Bill was an officer who was accused by a higher ranking and influential Marine of trying to send automatic weapons back to the United States to be sold on the street. In fact, it was the accuser who was sending the weapons home. None of the medals he was awarded, the letters of commendation he'd earned, the lives he'd saved, or the missions he'd accomplished made any difference in the court martial. His brothers in arms stood up for him, the lawyer did his best without tarnishing his own career. In the end, he did five years of a seven-year stint in Fort Leavenworth for a crime he didn't commit, while the guilty man got away clean. After he was released from prison, having been stripped of his rank and dishonorably discharged, he'd found himself unable to find a job…any job. He'd been an infantry officer, a recon ranger, a trained killer. Those weren't skills he could fall back on with his discharge. He worked to clear his name, but with no money and no resources, it was futile.

Bill's parents were killed in a car accident while he was locked up, and he'd lost track of his sister, his only living relative. He felt that losing track of her was probably for the best. He didn't want her to see him like this. She'd always looked up to him, but now he feared she would be disappointed in how his life had turned out. How could he prove to family that he had nothing to do with it? How could he convince her with a conviction on his record? He'd traveled the world. He'd held the lives of his comrades in his hands. He'd been honored and decorated for bravery under fire. He'd received the Silver Star, the Bronze Star, the Good Conduct Metal, the Combat Action Medal, and two Purple Hearts. He commanded his squad through numerous combat missions. He was a respected man who worked hard for what he had, only to have it stolen from him. And now, he couldn't even get a decent job. He'd tried parking cars but couldn't get bonded. He'd tried flipping burgers but couldn't take orders from wet-behind-the-ears punks, fresh out of high school or college. He tried a multitude of menial jobs, all of which made him feel useless. Eventually, he just gave up. It wasn't in his nature to quit, but with the decks all stacked against him, what was he to do? He did the best he could with the cards he was dealt. "Adapt and overcome," he'd always said. So that's what he did. He held on to what he needed to survive and carved out a meager existence among the population of homeless who filled the dark corners of Tampa. He gave up hope of anything better and began to just exist.

"Yes, I was a Marine once," Bill said, looking out the window. "They say, 'Once a Marine, always a Marine,' but I don't feel much like a Marine anymore."

When Bill finished his story and half a box of doughnuts, he fell silent again, staring out the window with watery eyes. It tore him up to relive the tragedy his life had become. He'd gradually forgotten who he once was and had fallen into the rut that was his life. He was comfortable being a "nobody," just existing until it was his time to die.

****

Harry was speechless, as were the other patrons in the doughnut shop who had gotten caught up in the story. Harry noticed that the conversations around them had stopped. The people who had complained about Bill being there were now looking on him with pity. Harry knew there was a story to be told, but he had no idea how rough Bill's life had been. Harry stared at Bill, sitting quietly after telling of his misery and disgrace. He felt so sorry for him. He was also sorry that he'd dredged up all the painful memories and put Bill in such a sad state of mind.

Breaking the silence, Harry said, "That's quite a story."

The old man came back to the present and turned to look at Harry again.

"My life is simple, just the way I like it. I get up in the morning. I head to the corner and wait for the morning traffic. I usually get about twenty dollars or so. I get something to eat. Sometimes the guy from the bakery gives me some of the old doughnuts. I don't have any stress. I can usually scrape up something to eat throughout the day. I don't bother anyone. No one depends on me. I can't let anyone down."

Harry then asked, "Are you happy?"

Bill tried to brush off the tears on his face. "Happy?" he replied. "I wouldn't say I'm happy. I gave up. But there's a lot of peace in realizing that there's nothing you can do. And believe me, there is nothing I can do. It's out of my hands."

Harry felt it was time to go. He got up from the table, took a last sip of his coffee, took five twenty-dollar bills out of his wallet, and dropped them on the table in front of the broken man.

"Don't give up on yourself, Bill," Harry said. "Life can turn on a dime."

Bill looked at the money on the table, noticed the extra twenties, and then looked back at Harry.

Harry knew what he was thinking, and said, "You've earned it, Bill. I'm sorry I made you relive it."

He left Bill in the coffee shop and headed off to work.

Harry couldn't get the story off his mind. He arrived at his office, only to realize that he had no memory of the drive. He was totally preoccupied by the expression on Bill's face as he told his story. He'd gotten the answers he wanted, but he felt like he had violated Bill's privacy. His curiosity put the poor guy in a bad place, and he was sorry he had done so.

It was time to go through his list of tasks. He checked them off, one by one, until they were all completed. He was finished with half the day still ahead. He picked up the keys to the condo in the Cayman Islands, said his goodbyes, and was on his way. Their flight was in the morning, and he wanted to spend the rest of the day getting prepared for the trip.

When he arrived home, he found Beth in the bedroom. She'd obviously gone for a swim, and was wearing her white bathrobe. He marveled at her perfect body as she walked over to give him a kiss.

"The pool was awesome," she said.

"I knew you'd like it," he replied.

"Get everything done?" she asked, towel drying her hair.

"Everything's done."

"I need to do a little shopping before we go. Can I use the Mercedes?"

"Sure," he said, handing her the keys. "You don't want me to go with you?"

"No, baby. Relax, and I'll be back soon," she said as she hurried to get dressed.

For the first time since they'd met, he felt nervous. He was worried she might be meeting someone behind his back. He realized he was in love with her. This wasn't infatuation. It was love.

He swallowed his worries and said, "I'd like to go to our restaurant tonight. You interested?"

"Sure," she said, pulling on her boots. "I just have to go by the bank and pick up a few things. You need anything?"

"No, I'm good," he said, watching her pick up the elevator key and her purse. Then he added, "Just you."

She kissed him and whispered in his ear, "You've already got me, baby."

And with that, all his fears melted away. It was obvious that she loved him too.

Beth blew a kiss to Harry from the elevator as the doors closed. She leaned back against the handrail and smiled. She hadn't been this happy in years, if ever. She was in love with him, and she'd fallen hard. He was the whole package—handsome, caring, and confident, a fantastic companion and lover, generous and kind. What more could a girl want?

She never thought about the age difference; it didn't matter. In fact, she felt comforted by his age and experience. It made her feel safe somehow. She never questioned him, and he never gave her cause to. Beth decided Harry was the one, and if he were to ask, she would definitely marry him. She knew a good thing when she had it.

Beth slid into the driver's seat of the Mercedes. It was the first time she'd driven a car like this. The vehicle was sleek and powerful. Leather hugged her body as she adjusted the seat. She started the engine and, with the flip of a switch, the top folded back and stowed itself away. A quick adjustment to the mirrors and stereo and she was off.

She only had two stops to make, the bank for traveler's checks and the mall for a couple of last-minute purchases. Harry had done so much for her and she wanted to do something for him. Beth knew exactly what that was. Harry had mentioned the pictures in Stan's office to her. She was going to help him get his own pictures.

At the mall, she purchased a couple of new bathing suits. At a photography store, Beth approached the huge display of cameras. She was overwhelmed by the variety of styles, gadgets, lenses, and flashes. She was relieved when the salesman approached.

As Beth pondered the selection of cameras she noticed the salesman watching her. He ran his fingers through his well-groomed hair and it appeared he was undressing her with his eyes as he approached her.

"Can I help you find anything?" he asked.

"Yes, please," Beth answered, smiling at the young man.

The salesman had that look in his eye. Beth had seen it many times, usually from the young men at The Boiling Point. She'd learned to ignore it, and she knew just how to shut him down.

"I'm looking for a gift for my husband," she said. "We're going on vacation tomorrow."

"I think I can help you with that," the salesman said, abandoning his hopes and returning to his duties. "Do you see anything you like?"

"I don't really know what I'm looking for," she confessed. "I want something really nice. We're going to the Cayman Islands, so we'll be boating and spending time on the beach. I guess it should be waterproof. What do you think?"

"Digital?"

"Yes, I guess so. I really don't know."

"Will you be scuba diving?"

"I don't know. I guess so."

"Let me show you something I think he'll love."

The salesman led her through the maze of cameras and she selected a package she felt good about.

She had it wrapped and headed back to Harry's apartment. She couldn't wait to give it to him.

****

Harry used the time while Beth was shopping to pack. He seldom went anywhere. When he did, it was usually business, but he was a meticulous traveler. He always folded and properly packed everything to make use of every inch of his suitcase. He was anxious for Beth to get home. Get home? Get home. Yeah, he was hooked. He wanted her to move in, and he had a present for her. He looked at the box on the dresser. He'd bought her a piece of jewelry, the first, and he couldn't wait to see her face when she opened it.

He heard the elevator doors slide open and the rustling of shopping bags. Hiding the velvet-covered box behind his back, Harry headed for the living room.

When Harry entered the room, he found Beth with the packages she'd bought. She was smiling and almost jumping up and down in anticipation.

As he approached, he took the box from behind his back. They smiled as they realized that each had a surprise for the other. They exchanged gifts.

"You go first," Harry said.

Beth opened her box and found a beautiful tennis bracelet. Smiling, she kissed Harry.

"Thank you, baby. It's beautiful," she said, putting the bracelet on her wrist. She wrapped her arms around his neck and hugged and kissed him again. "I love it!"

She admired the bracelet for a moment, then motioned to the package in his hands and said, "Your turn."

Harry opened the oversized package and was amazed. It was full of camera gear. He'd never owned a camera before, at least not a camera like this. It was perfect. He instantly thought of Stan's photos. Now he would have pictures for his office. He reached in the box and pulled out a clear container that looked a little like a display case for the camera. He looked confused, and then it came to him. It was a waterproof case. Harry's face lit up.

"It's for scuba diving," she beamed.

"Scuba diving," he said. "This is fantastic!" he added, as he rooted through the box. He'd always wanted to try scuba diving, and it hadn't occurred to him that this would be a perfect time. He spread the gear out on the table to get a good look at it all. Beth had chosen well. He had everything he needed to be a photographer.

"Baby, this must have cost you a fortune," he said, looking closely at the expensive gift.

"Hellooo!" she said, twisting her wrist back and forth to show off her new bracelet. "Besides, you're worth it." She was reaching into another bag. "And you'll need it to make me look good in this," she added, displaying a yellow T-back bikini. "And this," pulling a black one-piece out of the bag.

"Wow," Harry muttered as he looked at the bathing suits. "It's definitely time to test this equipment out," he said, fumbling with the camera.

"And now ladies and gentlemen, the moment you've been waiting for. The swimsuit competition!" Harry said, imitating a beauty pageant emcee.

Beth was giggling and running for the bedroom. "Which one first?"

"Surprise me," Harry yelled back, while attempting to mount a lens onto the camera body.

After a couple of minutes that seemed like an eternity, Beth emerged in Harry's oversized bathrobe. She was walking like a model down a runway. When she reached the middle of the room, she slowly opened the robe and held it as wide as her arms could reach. She was wearing the yellow T-back. The top accentuated her natural and very ample breasts. Her gentle curves were like poetry in motion. She had a tan that showed off the yellow suit as if it were fluorescent. She let the robe hit the floor and strutted around the room, turning and teasing, showing off all her assets. Her hair bounced lightly with each step, and as she turned to show off the T-back, she bent forward, hands on knees and her back slightly arched, then looked at Harry over her shoulder. She had to clear her throat to remind Harry to take a few pictures.

Harry had totally forgotten about the camera, but after her subtle hint, his attention was hurriedly redirected to it. Looking through the eyepiece, he snapped some shots, hoping the camera was adjusted somewhere close to what it should be. With every snap, Beth changed poses—first to one side, then the other, and finally facing straight toward him with both hands behind her head, pulling her luscious hair forward so all he could see were her sexy, pouty lips. With the last snap of the camera, she grabbed the robe from the floor and headed back to the bedroom.

Harry enjoyed the show and was sorry it was over, but his disappointment was short-lived as he remembered there was still one more suit to go. He quickly grabbed the camera and instruction manual, trying to make sure it was set for her next appearance. He had hoped she would save the skimpy yellow suit for last. After all, what could be sexier than a T-back? But that question was soon answered, and in a big way.

The door to the bedroom opened and Beth called out, "Are you ready?"

"Ready," Harry responded as he brought up the camera, looked through the eyepiece, and braced himself.

Beth emerged from the bedroom for the second time in the bathrobe, but this time her arms were not in the sleeves, and she was wearing black stilettos that laced up her delicate ankles. As she reached the center of the room, she threw her arms back and head forward, sending the robe flying back and her hair forward. In that instant, Harry realized she'd saved the best for last.

The black one-piece was very skimpy, not much more than a thin strip that started as a bikini bottom and ended up as two strips extending over her breasts and tying around the back of her neck. Black strings were woven from front to back on the sides, and a small string between her breasts kept everything in place.

She looked at Harry, her hair covering one eye, her lips slightly parted, with an expression that, without question, told Harry, "I want you now!" And with that, the fashion show started again.

Beth used the room as her runway, and Harry snapped picture after picture. She posed against the bar, on the floor, twisting and turning, and finally crawled up to Harry on her hands and knees like a cat on the prowl.

Harry was overcome with passion, and as she approached, he lowered the camera and watched her stand.

Beth, also caught up in the moment, took the camera from Harry with one hand and, with the other, reached behind her neck and untied the suit, letting the top drop to reveal her erect nipples. Then, with one smooth move, she placed the camera on the table and pressed her body against his. She squeezed him tightly, and they kissed.

There was no free will at this point. They were both victims of desire and could not stop, even if they wanted to. She wanted him, and he wanted her; it was as simple as that. There was no uncertainty, no awkwardness, only lust.

Harry put his strong arms around her and pulled her tightly against him as their tongues explored each other's mouths. Nothing was said, and nothing needed to be said. Their bodies did the talking.

Harry felt her squirming in his grip as she struggled to remove the bathing suit while maintaining the kiss. She reached down to release the strap on one of the shoes, but Harry stopped her.

"Leave those on."

She smiled, and they resumed the foreplay. She unbuckled his belt and fumbled to unzip his pants. Harry kicked off his shoes and, after unbuttoning his shirt, she stopped him, saying, "Leave that on."

Harry stopped for a second, then immediately picked her up. She wrapped her legs around his waist and her arms around his neck. The predator carried his prey to the nearest wall and pressed her against it, adjusting his hands until he was holding her by her hips. Then, with her back pressed firmly against the wall, he slowly entered her.

Beth gasped with pleasure. The feeling of the wall against her back and the unstoppable force penetrating her was irresistible. She felt captured. With all his attention, she was the sole object of his desire, and loved it.

Harry felt the sharpness of her stilettos against his back as he pressed into her, but the slight pain only added to his excitement.

Beth had her arms around Harry's neck as he drove her harder and harder against the wall with each thrust. The lovers increased the rhythm until, just before they climaxed, Harry stopped.

Harry's lover looked at him, on the verge of orgasm herself, her face filled with intense, sexual frustration. She held on tightly while being carried through the hallway to the bedroom with him still inside her, was laid gently on the bed, and then they finished what they'd started. The break in the action intensified their reward and they lay together afterwards, out of breath and out of strength.

Chapter Eight

The couple arrived in Fort Lauderdale, Florida, in the early evening. They took a cab to the yacht club that housed the company's yacht. It was the same yacht Stan fished from in the pictures hanging in Heather's office. The fact that they'd be using the same vessel, sleeping in the same bunk, and relaxing in the same salon, added to Harry's feeling that he had truly arrived. He was accepted among the highest figures in the company.

Dividends was a seventy-two-foot Sportfish, with all the bells and whistles, including its own captain and first mate. A person could live aboard her indefinitely. She was impeccably maintained and completely self-contained. Almost a quarter of a football field long, sparkling white, with polished hardware, a full tuna tower, and a custom fishing chair, she was the definition of luxury as well as functionality.

Beth marveled at the craft as a work of art. "Is this it?" she asked, not believing her eyes.

"This is it," Harry replied. "What do you think?"

"It's beautiful. Is it all for us?"

"It is."

As they looked from the dock, the first mate, Tyler, hurried over to welcome them and take their bags.

Tyler was a friendly young man in his twenties, all sinew and grizzle from working hard on this large boat and many before it. The work was difficult and demanding. There was always something to service, or repair, or replace, or polish. It was a full-time job, a job so big a second mate was needed, but there was no second mate. Tyler took care of *Dividends*. He had once told the captain he figured he would spend more time fixing mistakes made by someone who didn't love her the way he did. The captain and company decided to let him do it all himself. Besides, the vessel spent most of its time in port, only venturing out when the owners wanted to take a fishing trip or impress an important client. The rest of the time it was either at the dock, or on a short shake-down cruise to keep the barnacles off her keel. It wasn't as hard to maintain since it wasn't used too often.

"Hi, you must be Harry," Tyler said as he took Harry's hand. "Tyler."

"Hello, Tyler," Harry said, then introduced Beth.

"Pleased to meet you, Beth," he said, taking her hand.

"You too, Tyler," she replied.

Tyler reached for their bags. "Let me take those. Come on, welcome aboard." He turned to make his way down the dock, the heavy suitcases weightless in his strong hands.

Beth had seen his type before; she'd dated them in the past. She found it interesting to see him and Harry side by side. They were total opposites. There was a time when she would have been interested in this guy—before she met Harry, of course. She thought it odd that he didn't give her the looks she was used to getting from such guys, but chalked it up to professional conduct. Not ogling the guest's wives or girlfriends was probably a good idea if you're about to be in tight quarters with each other for extended periods of time. It was a big boat, but it would get small if personal conflicts arose.

Tyler took the luggage to the master cabin that would be home for this leg of their vacation. The boat was big, but the corridors were tight, and they had to step around each other as Tyler showed them the room's amenities. They included a queen-sized bed, a private head with shower, and everything else a person could want. The wall behind the bed was mirrored, which made the room look bigger than it was. There was a TV on the bulkhead opposite the bed and a stereo built into the cabinet below it.

"The captain will be back soon. Is there anything I can get for you?"

"No, Tyler, thank you," Beth said, taking his hand again. "We just want to settle in and unpack."

Tyler excused himself, and they were alone. They quickly unpacked and lay down together on the bed. They sighed and, for the first time since they left, they were relaxed. The quiet of the room was a welcome change for Harry, but apparently not for Beth.

It wasn't long before she asked, "Want to get out of here?"

Harry turned to her. "Where do you want to go?"

"Let's take a walk, explore the town, maybe have a drink."

Harry didn't say a word. He just rolled off the bed and onto his feet. He put on some comfortable shoes and a tropical shirt, donned his sunglasses and a ball cap, and was ready to go.

Beth chuckled. She had never seen him dressed like this. He always dressed for success and seeing him in full vacation mode was a big change. She grabbed her purse, and they left the boat.

Tyler was on the flybridge and noticed the couple leaving. He didn't say anything, but noted the direction they were headed and went back to his work.

As the two walked down the dock together, Harry with his hands in his pockets, Beth held his arm. Walking in step, they absorbed the setting sun and the gentle wind, and really started to unwind. Turning right, the couple headed down South Atlantic Boulevard. It was a vacation paradise. On their left were the beach and the beautiful Atlantic, and to the right were little shops and bistros as far as the eye could see. They wandered around the shops and, on the return trip, ended up in a small pub not too far from where *Dividends* was moored. It was a clean, quiet, dimly lit little place with a mixed clientele.

Sitting at a table near some tinted windows gave their feet a rest. It didn't seem possible, but they'd walked the strip for hours, and it was getting late. The sun had long since set, and the streets were busier than ever. Harry ordered beers and the two were enjoying the evening when three men walked in from the street.

The three were what Harry's mother always referred to as "hoodlums," and he kept an eye on them without being too obvious. They were loud, annoying, and obviously drunk. With their motorcycle jackets, boots, and chains attached to their wallets, it was obvious what they were. They went to the bar, ordered beer, then settled at a corner table where they leaned back in their chairs and continued to annoy the other patrons.

Beth didn't seem bothered by them. She just spoke a little louder, but Harry became agitated. He didn't want to start any trouble, but he was tired of the noise.

Beth glanced in their direction, still smiling from talking with Harry, and that was all it took.

One of the bikers noticed the beautiful bombshell from across the room. Harry noticed the biker's eyes lock on Beth. It looked like he was thinking of undressing her and molesting her. The expression on his face was pure lust. As his companions carried on, he sat quietly, staring and lusting.

Harry saw what was getting ready to play out. His eyes were locked on the predator and he knew where this was going. "Let's go," he said to Beth. She, not knowing what was happening, grabbed her bag and stood.

That was the spark needed to start the fire. The punk suddenly stood up and made his way across the bar toward Beth. When he did, his companions stopped their banter and paid attention to their companion's situation. As he approached, Harry sprang to his feet and stepped between them.

The punk slowed down when he saw how big Harry was. He didn't look very intimidating sitting across the room in a tourist shirt, but standing there in front of him, he was huge. But the play was in motion, and honor demanded he see it through. The punk was pretty big himself, and he had two buddies to back him up.

Beth suddenly became aware of the conflict, as did the other patrons. She moved behind Harry as he squared off with the punk. Harry didn't say a word, he just stood his ground.

"What's the problem, buddy?" the punk asked. "I just wanted to meet your daughter there," he said, turning halfway toward his buddies so they could hear the slam to Harry's age.

They busted into laughter at the remark, still leaning back in their chairs. They were used to people cowering at their feet because of their appearance and numbers.

As the biker turned, Harry shoved Beth back and away from him to gain fighting room. It had been a long time since he'd last had to fight. He was tough, but he was also twice as old as this bastard. He was counting on strength and experience to beat youth and numbers. He wouldn't have long to wait.

The punk turned back quickly and threw a right hook, trying to catch Harry off guard, but Harry was ready for it. He ducked below the haymaker, and countered with a powerful left jab to the ribs, just under the arm. As his attacker winced in pain, Harry caught him with an uppercut that lifted him off his feet and drove him back and to the floor. The fight was on.

The other punks sprung to their feet. They were moving to circle around Harry. One of them broke a beer bottle on the back of a chair as he approached.

Harry wasn't worried about the one on the floor. He'd always had a crushing right hand and felt something give way in the punk's jaw. He was out of the fight. But the other two could be a problem. Harry tried to keep from getting caught between them. He moved left, toward the one with the bottle; he didn't want the other to be able to make him a helpless target for his buddy's new weapon. Harry picked up a chair by its back and held it up defensively. All it would take would be the crashing blow of the chair to take one of them out of the fight, and then the other would be no problem. As they started to move in, Harry noticed a blur out of the corner of his eye. That blur was Tyler as he raced in and plowed into the punk on Harry's right, knocking him to the floor and pouncing on him. The punk was caught off guard and completely at the mercy of Tyler who showed none. The hard work of a life at sea had made Tyler too much for the thug to handle. Tyler held the punk by the lapel of his leather jacket with his left hand while pummeling his face with his right fist.

Quickly, Harry turned to the other hoodlum but stopped as he saw what was playing out. The guy to Harry's left looked at his partner getting his face pounded and was about to jump in to help. Things changed with the unmistakable click of the hammer of a stainless steel forty-five automatic that was pressed against the last thug's right temple. The brawler froze, motionless, losing control of his bladder, soaking his jeans.

"Think about it," an unfamiliar woman's voice said confidently. "I think it's time for you to leave."

He dropped the beer bottle and ran out of the bar, having forgotten about his buddies.

Harry put down the chair, grabbed the guy with the broken jaw, dragged him to his feet, and threw him out the front door. Tyler and his victim followed.

The patrons of the bar stood and applauded them, and the trio took that as a cue to leave before the police showed up. Harry led Beth out of the battle zone. They were near the door when Harry said, "Glad you happened by when you did, Tyler." Then turning to the mysterious woman, "And you, too."

"Harry, I'd like you to meet your captain, Maria Sanchez," Tyler said with pride.

Maria Sanchez was a middle-aged woman, physically fit and tanned from years on the water. She was not at all what

Harry expected, but she was a third-generation captain. Her father taught her everything he knew about fishing as his father had him, and she was one of the best in the area. She'd earned her place on *Dividends*. She was an attractive woman with a heart of gold and self-confidence you could hear in her every word.

"Nice to meet you, Ms. Sanchez," Harry said.

Maria slid her pistol back into its holster in the back of her pants, pulling her shirt over the grip to conceal it, and took his hand. "Maria," she corrected.

Harry introduced Beth, and they all started back to the yacht.

****

Harry sat on the flybridge with a margarita in his hand. Maria was to his right, also enjoying a drink. The evening breeze was coming in from the east, and the cool salt air coming off the Atlantic was refreshing. They sat together, enjoying the night, while Beth took a shower in the master's quarters. From this vantage point, they could see for miles in all directions. The lights of the strip illuminated the coastline, defining the border between the land and the sea. It appeared that the world just dropped off into nothingness except for the boats. There were precious few boats out to sea that night, and red, green, and white lights gave away their positions in the darkness, clumped together like tiny, colorful fireflies.

"So, Harry, what kind of adventure are you looking for?" Maria asked.

"You mean other than the one tonight?" Harry retorted.

"You handled yourself pretty well," she said. "I think you broke that guy's jaw."

"Oh, darn," Harry replied sarcastically "He had it coming."

Taking a sip from her drink, Maria said, "No argument from me," adding, "What do you want to do while you're here? Tuna, marlin, cruising—what's your pleasure?"

"What do you suggest?" Harry asked.

"It's your vacation, Harry. You have *Dividends* at your disposal. Make use of her. What do you want to do?"

"I want to catch a trophy. I think a marlin would look good in my office, but I'm not sure about a tuna."

"We can do that," she said.

"I'd like to cruise to the Bahamas, too," he added.

"It's settled then. Tomorrow, we'll set out in search of the big blue marlin. Then, when we've landed your trophy, it's off to the Bahamas."

"What about supplies?" Harry asked.

"This is your vacation, Harry. Let us worry about that. We stocked up when we were told you were coming. Don't worry, we have it covered."

After a few moments of silence, the door to the salon on the main deck opened and Beth came out in her robe, her hair in a towel.

Maria motioned to her. "So what's her story?" she asked.

"She's the love of my life," he said.

"A little young, isn't she?" Maria smiled.

"True love knows no age," he replied, looking down at Beth.

Beth looked around briefly, then noticed Harry on the bridge and waved.

"She's a lucky girl," Maria said with a touch of envy.

Harry replied, without acknowledging the compliment, "I'm the lucky one."

At that moment, Tyler came down the dock with a duffle bag and some personal gear.

"What's his story?" Harry asked as he watched the young man come aboard and greet Beth. He felt a twinge of jealousy as they spoke quietly and then laughed.

"Tyler?" Maria laughed. "You don't have to worry about him."

"What do you mean," he asked.

"You can't tell?" Maria asked.

"Tell what?" Harry asked.

Maria leaned slightly toward Harry and whispered, "He's gay."

"You're kidding."

"He's more likely to make a move on you than on her," she retorted.

"Wow. I'd never have thought it after today."

"He's gay, not a wimp," she said with pride, "and he's one hell of a first mate."

Harry leaned over to Maria and quietly whispered, "Don't tell Beth."

"What do you mean?"

"She doesn't understand why he hasn't hit on her," he explained. "Let's let it be our little secret."

"You're terrible." Maria took another sip and chuckled. "This is going to be quite a trip."

Chapter Nine

The next morning, they set to sea long before daylight. Maria and Tyler quietly prepped *Dividends* and got her under way without waking the guests. Harry and Beth slept as the massive twin V-8 engines growled in the engine room and slowly pushed the boat forward. The gentle movement of the seventy-two-foot hull and the rhythmic drone of the engines kept them asleep as *Dividends* worked its way on the long, slow journey through the many channels leading to the pass and out to sea. When the engines were pushed up to twenty-one hundred rpm, the gentle drone became a synchronized roar accompanied by the distinctive whistles of the twin turbochargers on each of the huge power plants. The cabin tilted aft as the bow rose and the vessel began to plane. The couple woke and, throwing on some clothes, made their way to the deck.

Once outside, the world seemed completely different from the night before. The deck that had been so easy to walk was now tilted aft, making it hard to keep footing without holding onto the handrails. Maria was on the bridge, at the helm; Tyler was nowhere in sight. Harry and Beth climbed the flybridge ladder and joined their captain. It was an impressive sight, this big piece of machinery, more like a small house than a boat, roaring and gliding along at speeds greater than twenty-five knots under the fingertip control of a smaller-than-average woman. She looked as though she was driving a small sedan on a country road, not the slightest bit intimidated. And why should she be? She'd done this a thousand times before and sometimes in fearsome weather.

On the front deck, Tyler stood, wind blowing through his hair, totally at home on the deck, his sea legs keeping him perfectly balanced. He was tending to his work on this boat he loved so much: stowing the fenders and locking them down, securing the mooring and the spring lines, making sure the hatches on the foredeck were secured in case of bad weather. One last check of the dinghy's hold-down straps completed his routine. When he was finished, he looked up to the bridge, letting the captain know he was heading back to the cockpit. They worked together like a well-oiled machine.

It was important for Maria to know where Tyler was at all times. The transition from foredeck to cockpit was dangerous, and with one misstep, a person could end up overboard. At twenty-five knots, if she didn't know someone was missing, that person would be dead.

When Tyler looked up at the bridge, he saw Harry and Beth. He smiled and waved and began making his way back.

Beth waved back to him and turned to Harry who was smiling slyly at her. "Don't worry, baby, he could never replace you." She was happy he was finally noticing her. She'd been thinking she was losing her appeal.

"You sure?" he asked as he looked at Maria, smiling at the inside joke. "He might just be smitten with you."

"No way, I know what I have."

Both Maria and Harry laughed to themselves.

Beth, not getting the joke, took Harry's hand and said, "I'm serious."

"OK," he said, still smiling. "I believe you."

Maria didn't say a word. She just enjoyed the joke silently.

They powered on for another half hour, and then Maria gradually pulled back the throttles. The whistle of the turbochargers subsided, the engines quieted down to a dull drone, and the vessel settled down again to a slow lumbering. It was time to fish.

Tyler came out of the salon with two huge deep-sea rods, each with a matching gold anodized reel. He placed one in the rod holder on the right side of the fighting chair bolted to the deck and the other on the left. Maria deployed the outriggers from each side of the bridge. They automatically locked in the outward position. Tyler motioned for Harry to come down from the bridge.

Maria set the controls to neutral and began the climb up the ladder to the control station at the top of the tuna tower. There, she shifted into forward and started a slow troll as she scanned the horizon for a sign of the elusive blue marlin.

Tyler started a chum trail, tossing a mixture of menhaden oil and ground-up baitfish plus "a few secret herbs and spices," as he liked to call them, overboard to draw in the prey. The first mate then rigged the lines and dropped them overboard to begin the day's fishing. The outriggers pulled them a good thirty feet away from the boat on each side, widening the fishing area. He let them out a distance away from the boat and locked the reels. Then he brought out another one, rigged it, and placed it in the center rod holder on the transom. This one he only let out about one hundred feet, straight back in the prop wash. He then motioned for Harry to sit in the chair.

Harry felt like a king as he sat in the huge, luxurious chair. Beth was by his side, as they waited for the action to start. This was Harry's world, not hers. She was more into the sun and wind. After a short time with no excitement, she got bored, so she changed into the t-back bathing suit and went up to the foredeck where Tyler had set up a cushion for her to sun herself. She lay down on her stomach and pulled her hair off her back. Then she untied her top so she would have no tan lines.

Maria looked down from the tower and, seeing all the exposed skin, yelled down to Tyler to go put some sunscreen on her.

Hearing this, Beth was conflicted. She didn't want to do anything that would jeopardize her relationship with Harry, but she wanted this young man to pay attention to her. So when Tyler showed up on the deck with the sunscreen, she reluctantly let him apply it. Tyler knelt next to her and applied the sunscreen like a masseuse. The creamy lotion cooled her skin, but it was not the way she thought it would be. Even when he applied it to her legs and her semi-naked ass, it was very professional and unemotional, leaving her feeling as if it had been done by a hospital nurse instead of a virile young man. Then, as quickly and efficiently as he started, he was finished and gone. He hurried back to the cockpit and the fishing.

Over the next few hours, they trolled the baits and waited for a strike. As the tide receded, they quit and reeled in the lines. Maria would wait for the next incoming tide, when she seemed to have better luck fishing, although it shouldn't make much difference this far out to sea.

They secured everything and went into the comfort of the air conditioned salon to cool off and have an early dinner. They were many miles from any obstacle, and it would have been OK to let the boat drift, but it was easy enough to pay out the anchor and secure the boat. This was Tyler's time to relax a little. He wasn't much of a cook, so it was up to Maria to come up with dinner, something she enjoyed doing.

Sitting around the table after dinner, they all agreed they'd had enough for one day and decided to wait until morning to try again. Then, after the sun had set, the only lights that could be seen, except the ones from *Dividends,* were the moon and the stars. The world became profoundly quiet. There wasn't a ripple on the water, which reflected the moonlight almost perfectly. They all walked out on the deck to admire the stars. They were brilliant in the night sky, unaffected by city lights or pollution. It was hard to believe that the light that they were seeing had left those stars thousands of years before. It was as if they were lit just for them on that night. Then Maria turned out all the lights except one anchor light at the top of the tuna tower and shut down the generator. The night became more deeply surreal. No noise, no wind, no ambient light—just the moon and stars and their reflections on the water.

Beth clung to Harry, and he put his arm around her, pulling her closer. She looked up at him and said, "Thank you for bringing me here." She realized this was something she never would have done if not for Harry.

Maria and Tyler sat quietly on the flybridge and watched the couple bathed in the moonlight.

"It wouldn't be the same without you," he told her. As his eyes began to adapt to the ultra-dim light, he looked at her, seeing the stars mirrored in her beautiful eyes. He realized how precious she was to him, how she filled his soul.

They quietly held each other. In the darkness and quiet, everything else faded away until it was just the two of them in the serene world…and finally…a kiss.

****

By the next morning, Harry and Beth felt much more at home on the water. The boat was surprisingly comfortable and not as claustrophobic as they thought it might be. It actually seemed roomy once they got used to it. By the time the two climbed out of bed, Maria had breakfast ready. The spacious galley was like the kitchen in a small apartment and made meal preparation pretty easy.

Tyler used the time to prepare the boat for the day's fishing. It took a lot to ensure that the boat was ready, starting with the usual chore of checking the oil in the engines, transmissions, and generator. It required him to crawl into the cramped engine compartment which was located under the main salon of the vessel. There was a lot to check: sea strainers for raw water pumps, fuel filter sediment bowls, and drive belts to name a few. Things that can't be taken for granted. The seas might turn rough with no notice and and the crew and passengers would count on each and every system to keep them alive. It was time consuming, and Tyler always got up extra early to attend to it. But for him, it was a labor of love. It was clear Tyler loved the boat…and his job.

Once the mental checklist was complete, Tyler prepped the deck. He wiped the morning dew from the fighting chair and the gunwales, the ladder leading to the flybridge. He brought out the rods from their racks in the salon and placed them strategically in the holders in the cockpit. Frozen squid was brought out to thaw and the lines were prepared. As the sun cleared the horizon, *Dividends* was ready for action.

By the time the clients came out of the salon, well fed and ready to fish, the anchor was stowed, the lines were in the water, and the boat was in a slow troll. It wasn't long before the morning bite arrived, and the magic words were yelled that started the chaos that marlin fishing really is.

"Fish on!" Tyler yelled up to the bridge. The line from the outside string of the port outrigger released itself from the clip, and the battle began.

Maria slowed the boat, turned herself around, and stood backward at the helm so she could watch what was going on in the cockpit. Tyler took the rod and put it in the gimbal at Harry's feet. Then he and Beth began the frantic race to bring in all the other lines so they would not foul the one in play. When the last one was in, Harry began to retrieve line. It was a back-and-forth fight that took the better part of an hour, and when it was won, it was lost. It wasn't a blue marlin; it was a large mako shark. It had put up a hell of a fight, but it wasn't what they were looking for. Tyler reached over the side, cut the leader close to the hook, and the fish was gone.

"That's a good sign," Tyler said. "Where there're makos, there could be marlin."

All the lines were reset, and the process began again. It was perfect weather for fishing. The water was glassy calm, and it was easy to spot a marlin on the surface. Up in the tower, Maria scanned the water's surface in zones, looking for the fin of a blue marlin. Hours dragged by until she saw it, about a hundred yards off the starboard bow—a fully open fin with a tail following it. It was a marlin, and it was a big one. She maintained speed and course until the marlin was off the starboard beam, then she turned slightly to starboard to lead the baits over the area. She alerted Tyler and turned around in the tower again, standing backwards to watch the action. Harry was at the ready in the chair, and Beth and Tyler stood ready for action.

The fin showed up again, close to the line in the prop wash. It showed some interest, following the bait for a moment, then moving off to the side and reacquiring it again. Then it veered off and started off to port. Maria turned slightly to port to take the next set of baits over the fish. They didn't have long to wait.

****

Cruising through the surface water, the marlin was on the prowl for a meal. It kept its distance from the large creature moving along the surface. It was noisy and alien, but other than changing course slightly, it didn't seem to pursue him. There was a small fish following the creature. He tried to catch it, but lost sight of it in the turbulence. Then he saw it and tried again, but again lost sight of it in the wake of the big beast. He drifted off to find easier game. He maintained a slow prowl until he saw another fish headed straight for him. With some heavy kicks of his powerful tail he descended, circling, keeping the fish in sight. He came up behind it and with a mighty strike, engulfed the fish. It was a mistake.

****

The line on the inside clip of the outrigger pulled tight, and the clip released, signaling that the marlin had taken the bait. The slack on the line was quickly taken, and the fight was on again.

"Fish on!" Harry cried out.

Everyone scrambled. Beth and Tyler reeled in the other lines. Harry pulled the rod from the holder on the right side of the chair, slid it into the gimbal, and clipped it to the harness he was wearing. Maria slowed the boat to allow everyone to get the lines in, as well as to slow the stripping of the line from the reel with the great fish. Then the fight really began. Harry leaned back in the chair. The harness pulled the rod back as he cranked the reel. He leaned forward as he cranked in slack, then leaned back again to pull in more line. He repeated this cycle over and over as the marlin went from side to side.

The marlin was panicked, racing in one direction and then the other, pulling against the unseen force preventing escape. He tried diving deep into the dark abyss, then raced to the surface and breached, kicking and shaking his head. This seemed to provide some release, so he did it again and again, only to find the tension returning when he re-entered the water.

Harry watched with excitement as the marlin breached the water, trying to throw the bait from his mouth. It was a big one, easily seven hundred and fifty pounds. "Woooooooo!" he screamed. "Come on, baby. Come to papa!"

The marlin put up a powerful fight for over an hour. The closer he got to the boat, the harder he fought. This is where Maria's expertise came into play. Standing backward with the helm centered, she backed down on the fish, revving the engines in reverse in an effort to gain ground. Then, as they were close, she alternated the engines to keep the fish directly off the transom. When the fish finally surrendered to the invisible force it was battling, she closed the throttles and shifted into neutral. The slowing of the engines and lack of turbulence from the propellers seemed to calm the fish. Tyler opened the transom door and carefully tied a line to the tail, then to a hook attached to a block and tackle. The other end of the tackle was attached to a lifting eye on the leg of the tower. Then he pulled the big fish out of the water. The fight was over and the fish was muscled onto the deck through the transom door. Harry climbed out of the chair and knelt down next to it, holding the rod in his hand and posing for pictures. Tyler snapped several shots with Harry's new camera. They hurried, because they wanted to get the fish back into the water. There was no need to kill it. Harry called to Beth, and the two of them posed for one last quick shot with the fish.

Beth found herself feeling sorry for the fish. She was saddened at the thought of killing the innocent creature that was simply swimming free and minding its own business. The thrill of the whole thing ended with the lifting of the fish out of its element and onto the teakwood lined deck of the boat. The majesty and beauty of it was lost the moment it began to thrash helplessly out of the water. It was big and magnificent, and although a little scary, she didn't want it hurt.

The line holding it from the tail was cut. The marlin was pushed back out through the transom door and guided around to the side of the boat by the leader attached to the hook. Maria shifted the transmissions into forward and the boat started to move slowly forward, forcing water through the big fish's gills. At first, it seemed it had been out of the water too long. It was exhausted from the battle and had been unable to replenish its oxygen supply out of the water immediately after the fight.

Beth was on the verge of tears as she watched the lifeless body pulled along beside the boat. It slowly and lifelessly tilted over to one side as it was pulled through the water. But suddenly, it opened and closed its mouth and tried to resist again. At that, Tyler leaned over the gunwale and cut the leader, leaving the hook to rust away and the fish good as new, and maybe a little wary from the experience. Beth let out a sigh of relief as she saw the fish recover, and they all watched as it disappeared into the depths.

"I guess it's better this way," Harry confessed. "But I really wanted it mounted."

"It will be," Maria responded.

"How's that?" he asked.

"The fish doesn't need to be killed anymore. There are molds of all species and sizes now, and they can airbrush a fiberglass fish of the right size to match the pictures that you take. You get your mount, and the fish gets to live to fight another day. Everybody wins," she explained.

"Amazing," he replied.

"You want to give it a try, Beth?" Tyler asked.

"No, thank you. I'm about fished out," she said.

And with that, the fishing was over. Tyler cleaned and put away the gear, washed down the blood the marlin lost off of the deck, relocked the outriggers, and prepared the boat for cruising.

"So I guess we're headed to the Bahamas?" Beth asked.

"If that's what you want," Maria said. "But the Bahamas is a bit of a tourist trap."

"What do you suggest?" Harry asked.

"Well, you have *Dividends* at your disposal. You can take a cruise ship to the Bahamas another time. How about going somewhere other people can't go, a place you need a yacht to get to?"

"And you know of such a place?" Beth asked.

"I sure do," Maria said, as she reached for the GPS mounted in the console and scanned through the saved waypoints. "Conception Island."

"Conception Island," Beth repeated, laughing. "Sounds very fertile." She bumped hips with Harry. "Think we should go there, Harry?"

"Island, yes, but let's hold off on the conception," he said, grinning at her.

Maria smiled as she pushed the "Enter" button on the GPS and engaged the autopilot. "Well, we'll just see about that," she said, as the yacht took a slow turn onto the new course. She pushed the polished throttle levers forward smoothly and the engines once again roared and whistled. The boat planed out and the throttles were pulled back to take the pressure off the engines and continue a comfortable cruising speed. *Dividends* locked onto their heading, and in the day's failing light, they motored toward the isolated destination.

****

The evening was quiet and still. Maria and Tyler took turns at the helm after the long day of fishing. Harry was sore from the effort of cranking in the shark and the marlin. He and Beth went to sleep early. The day's events, the movement of the boat under their feet for the second day, and the gentle groan of the big engines were like a tranquilizer. At the moderate cruise speed, it took several hours to get there, but there was no hurry; it was too late to enjoy the island, and there was no reason to tax the engines.

They made it to Conception Island at a little past four a.m. Maria and Tyler anchored the boat and took turns sleeping. Harry and Beth slept through the night. When the engines were shut down and the only thing running was the small generator, they fell into an even deeper sleep.

Maria and Tyler were still taking turns sleeping and watching the boat. When in port it was safe for both of them to sleep, but out at sea, past the ten-mile limit, they were mostly in international waters. If something went wrong, or someone wanted to hijack the boat, their only defense would be self-defense, and to defend yourself, you need to see the danger approaching. The boat had plenty of weapons, including assault rifles, tucked away in a locker that was easy to get to, yet out of sight. But when only one of the crew was on guard out at sea, he or she wore a sidearm and had an assault rifle at hand. It was not only good practice, it was company orders.

Beth and Harry slept in until close to ten a.m. They woke up and made their way to the galley for coffee. Beth wore one of Harry's shirts, which covered her like an oversized robe. Harry wore swim trunks and a baseball cap. They were happy to find fresh coffee ready. The sun was high in the sky, bearing down on *Dividends*. The dinghy had been hoisted from the deck and was moored to a stern cleat. They sheltered their eyes from the sun as they walked out on deck.

"Good morning," they heard Maria call from the flybridge.

"Morning," Beth responded. "Is that the whole island?"

"That's it," Maria replied, as all three of them looked off the stern at the tiny paradise.

The island was a mile across, a pile of sand with trees and foliage, and about four miles of beaches. There were a few sailboats in the area, anchored well apart from each other and from *Dividends*. Beth could see a couple walking on the beach. She went into the salon and returned a moment later with a pair of binoculars. Raising them to her eyes, she saw something she didn't expect.

"Oh, my God!" she said, handing Harry the binoculars. "Take a look."

Harry took the binoculars and looked for himself. Gazing through the glasses, Harry saw what she was talking about. The couple was nude. They seemed to be the only couple on the island, as far as he could see. They were walking together without a care in the world, enjoying the midday sun on their naked bodies. "Oookay" Harry said, peering at them. "I see what you mean about a different kind of destination," he told Maria.

"Tyler can take you ashore when you're ready," Maria said. "Or you can take the dinghy yourself."

Beth had never been on a nude beach before. She was embarrassed and exhilarated at the thought. She had dreamed of the opportunity, but never thought she would get the chance for the experience.

"Let's have Tyler take us ashore after breakfast," Harry said. And with that, they went into the air-conditioned salon of the boat for brunch.

After eating, Beth changed into her black bathing suit and put on an oversized hat to protect her shoulders from the sun on the short boat ride to the island. She'd packed a small bag with the things they'd need for the day—bottled water, sandwiches, sunscreen, towels, and a book, among other things. Harry put on a shirt, sandals, sunglasses, and a straw hat, then considered himself ready. They climbed onboard the dinghy Tyler already had running and cast off.

The ride to the island was smooth. There was a slight wind, but *Dividends* was moored on the leeward side of the island where the water was smooth and flat. The thirteen-foot dinghy streaked across the water under the power of the twenty-five horsepower outboard. Tyler had been here many times before and knew just where to take them for some privacy. He maneuvered the dinghy through a shallow passage leading to a small lagoon deep in the center of the island. No one else was there, so they had the quiet, secluded beach, surrounded by trees, to themselves. Tyler eased the small craft onto the beach and they all got off.

"What do you think?" Tyler asked. "Like it?"

"It's beautiful!" Beth said excitedly.

"Great," Tyler replied, taking a couple of lounge chairs out of the dinghy. He set them on the beach along with the bag Beth had packed and a CD player and a small cooler with drinks. "How long would you like to stay?"

"Forever," Harry said, looking around.

Tyler handed him a two-way radio and showed him how to use it. "I'll be monitoring the radio. Call me if you need anything. If I don't hear from you, I'll be back in a few hours."

"You're leaving?" Beth asked.

"You don't need me in your way. This is your vacation. Besides, I'm only a radio call away," he replied, holding up another radio.

Tyler climbed back into the dinghy, powered back away from the island, and headed out the way he came. Soon the sound of the engine faded away, and they were alone. There were no sounds other than the calls of the birds that were native to the island.

Harry opened the lounge chairs, setting them up with the cooler between them. He fiddled with the CD player until it was playing soothing island music. Then he turned his attention to Beth, who had been making some preparations of her own. She had untied the top of the black bathing suit from behind her neck and let it slide down to her waist. She was pulling the rest of it off and was stepping out of it as he watched.

As she undressed, she felt a rush of excitement she hadn't felt since she undressed in front of a man for the first time. The idea of being naked, completely exposed to the world, in a place that was secluded, but not exactly private, was liberating and thrilling. She walked over to Harry and started to kiss him as she unbuttoned his loud, flowery tourist shirt. She pulled it over his shoulders and left it at his elbows, somewhat confining his arms. She then pulled down his swim trunks. He felt the rush, too, as his trunks hit the sand. It had been quite a while since they'd felt alone enough to make love. The boat was small, and although it was quiet in their cabin, they didn't feel it was private enough for intimacy, but this was different. They felt free, they felt alive, and they wanted each other. There was the sun, and the sand, the shade of the trees—and the love they felt for each other.

He removed his shirt then gently pulled Beth up by her shoulders and wrapped his arms around her, turning her to face away from him and capturing her arms in his. He nuzzled his face in her hair and nibbled her ear as he caressed her breasts. He blew into her ear, which gave her goose bumps all over her body. His hands skimmed her body with light taking touches that made her blood boil. She put her hand behind his neck as he was kissing hers, pulling him tighter and grinding back against him. At this point, it wouldn't have mattered if they'd been in a crowd of strangers; but it was just the two of them in this island paradise, and that was just the way they wanted it. He guided her to her knees, following her down, and then leaned her forward and onto her hands in front of him. She felt captured and controlled, and loved it. They felt like animals in the wild.

The smell of the ocean and the feeling of the sand on her legs and between her fingers reminded Beth where they were, and it added to the thrill. He then pushed deep inside her as she gasped with excitement. Holding her waist, he began to thrust, slowly and gently at first, then increasing in speed and intensity, overcome with passion. He let his hands slide gently up and down her back and across her shoulders. He felt her body begin the familiar movements that let him know she was nearing climax, so he slowed down, trying to prolong the experience. He reached forward and collected her hair in his left hand, holding her shoulder with his right. This was all she could stand. Her efforts to hold back the inevitable were lost as he began to pull her hair, gently at first, but harder and harder as he drove himself deeper and faster into her. She screamed aloud with pleasure. Hearing her orgasm was all he could stand, and he cried out as he joined her.

Afterwards, they collapsed together, trying almost in vain to catch their breath. As they lay there together, their bodies covered with sand clinging to the sweat on their bodies, they held each other tightly and, finally, began to breathe again. It was a powerful experience for them both, linking them to this location forever. They were hundreds of miles away from their lives, and eventually, they would go home. But part of them would always be here—here on this beach—this beach that would always keep their secret encounter just that, a secret.

****

Maria took the opportunity to unwind. With Tyler off the boat, she had a chance to be alone. She could let her hair down and relax in a way that, as the boat's captain, she couldn't normally. She liked being a captain, but she'd been making a living on the water since she was eighteen years old. In her youth, she worked on a commercial fishing boat; it was hard work and she enjoyed it. But when the opportunity came up to captain the seventy-two-foot *Dividends*, she jumped at the chance. She thought it was a dream job, an easy way to make a living. And it was easy, too easy. It was boring.

Maria missed the excitement of her previous job. Now she was a babysitter for rich people, trying to keep them entertained and out of trouble, then sitting in port waiting for the next group. She had twenty years on the water, fishing for a living, and the routine was getting old.

At thirty-eight, she wondered if her life was passing her by. There must be something else out there, but she didn't know what else to do. Being in charge was all she had known since she worked her way up from a deck hand and took the helm as captain. It was difficult for her to have a relationship, not only due to the work schedule, but because of being a control freak. A captain must be in control. He or she can't take anything for granted, but that makes for strained personal relationships. She was already at an age when it might be difficult to start a family, and there was no one special in her life. She was at a point where she needed to make some real choices.

And then there was Tyler. He was young, and although he was a good first mate, she worried what would happen to him if she left the job. Some captains bring their own crew, so he would probably lose his job if she were to leave, and he loved *Dividends*. He would make a good captain someday, but he was too young for the company to give him the position now. So, at least for now, she would stay.

Tyler approached in the dinghy after dropping off their guests. She smiled as he tied the dinghy to the stern cleat and came aboard. She found it difficult to live onboard with him. After all, she was a woman, and he was a man—a sexy man. He always wore a shirt when they had clients, but when they were alone, he usually went without. With his rock-hard abs and muscular legs teasing her, it was frustrating. *If he were straight,"* she thought silently, *"this would be a dream job.* That wasn't the case, and it wasn't his fault. Maria was the captain, he was the first mate, and that was the end of it. But she often fantasized about having him. In some of those moments when she was alone and could let her hair down, she would have imaginary encounters with him, satisfying herself in the process. It was all harmless, and after all, she was a woman and had needs, but when Tyler was around, it was hard not to cross the line. And then as she watched the young man lean over as he tied the dingy to the stern cleat, his tan body glistening with sweat, totally unaware of her hidden lust for his body, she felt guilty. Like a predator stalking its prey. She felt the frustration of wanting something that she couldn't have. Life could be so unfair.

"I left them in the lagoon," Tyler told Maria.

"They'll like that," she replied. She pictured herself there. Not as a captain, but as a guest, with someone else to worry about the details. "Maybe someday," she muttered under her breath.

"What?" Tyler asked.

"Nothing," she replied.

"OK," he said, and with that he was off to the never-ending job that was *Dividends*. He disappeared through a hatch in the deck, attending to his work.

"So unfair," she muttered.

****

The day in the lagoon was a feast for their senses. Harry and Beth stretched out in the lounge chairs, covered with suntan lotion, listening to the birds and for the sound of the dinghy approaching. They figured they'd have enough time to dress when they heard that sound.

Harry thought about how this came to be. He was so alone a short time ago, just working and sleeping, but now he was living, reaping the rewards of his labors and doing so with a beautiful woman who was also a great companion. He looked over at her, lying on the lounger, her naked body eagerly absorbing the sun. He couldn't help but wonder, "What does she see in me?" In his eyes, he was an old man—eighteen years her senior. The punk in the bar pointed that out just before he hit the floor. "Just wanted to meet your daughter," he'd said. It was meant as an insult, but it could be true. Harry was just old enough to be her father. It was obvious she loved him, but what would it be like as they aged together?

Beth was suddenly startled by the sound of an outboard motor approaching. He hadn't heard it. He was too engrossed in his own thoughts. They both raced to shake the sand out of their bathing suits and put them on. That's when Beth realized how much quicker her un-tanned skin soaked up the tropical sun. She winced as she pulled the straps up and over her breasts, struggling to adjust it over the tender skin. She shook out her hair and put on her big hat and sunglasses.

It was easier for Harry. He slid on his trunks and was ready to go, just as the dinghy came into view.

There was Tyler, powering toward them in the little boat. It seemed like no time had passed since he dropped them off, but it had been more than five hours. The sun was only three hours from the horizon, and it was time to go. He nosed the dinghy up on shore and killed the engine as Harry and Beth gathered their belongings and headed for the water taxi.

"Need a lift?" Tyler shouted from the driver's seat. He jumped out, collected the lounge chairs and Beth's bag, and stowed them in the vessel. He then turned to help Beth into the dinghy.

Harry climbed in and took a seat.

In one smooth motion, Tyler shoved the boat backwards, climbed in, started the engine, and began to back out. "So how was your day?" Tyler asked the tired-looking couple. "Did you have fun?"

"Yes, it was wonderful," Beth responded while looking at Harry.

"It sure was," Harry said softly.

Tyler smiled and shifted the boat into forward.

Beth and Harry stared at the beach they now knew so intimately, watching as it became smaller. It was as though they were leaving an old friend behind, an old friend that would forever keep their visit secret. As the boat spun around, they silently said goodbye, wanting to stay in this paradise forever, yet knowing they would probably never return. And it wouldn't be the same the second time around. It was a-once-in-a-lifetime experience, trying to re-live it would only cheapen the memory. Five hours in paradise, a segment of time that passed in the blink of an eye. Instinct and emotion guided their actions that day, neither of them knowing what to expect. Were they to try to live it again, it would be like acting in a play, both of them following an agenda. And now, as the spot on the beach disappeared forever from their view, it went softly from reality to memory, and there it would fondly remain.

****

They'd been at Conception Island for more than a week, swimming in the surf, walking the beaches, and fishing the clear waters. The four sat on the back of *Dividends*, relaxing in the failing light, when they noticed an inflatable raft with two women aboard approaching from another yacht. It eased up next to the dinghy still tied at the transom. Maria watched the approach with her hand on the grip of her pistol. She didn't have a reason to think they meant any harm, but it never hurt to be cautious. One of them could have stood up with an assault rifle and turned a beautiful evening into a nightmare. Better to be ready for anything.

"What can we do for you?" Maria asked.

"We wanted to invite you all to a beach party tonight," said one of the women from the raft. "Some of us are leaving in the morning when the wind picks up, and we want to invite everyone to join us for dinner and a bonfire on the beach before we go."

"Sounds good," Harry replied. "What do we need to bring?"

"It's a potluck," the other woman added. "Just bring whatever you like."

"See you there," Beth said as they watched them pull away and head to the next boat in the cove.

Maria relaxed her grip on the pistol as they motored away. Party or not, she wasn't about to leave the boat. If the clients wanted to leave, that would be their choice, but she was responsible for the security of the vessel and would be staying onboard.

Harry and Beth went below to get out of the heat and take a nap. They expected to be out late, and it had been an eventful day. This party sounded like the perfect end to the first leg of their vacation. They went below and cuddled up together on the bed to rest.

****

Up on deck, Maria and Tyler sat together in the twilight, an old routine for them. Tyler sat in the second seat on the bridge next to Maria, his shirt off, his tanned six-pack abs glistening with sweat. He liked working with his captain. She earned his respect every day. She was his captain, mentor, boss, and in some ways, his mother. There was nothing he wouldn't do for her. She was twice his age and certainly not his type, but he did love her.

Maria, sitting in her captain's chair, looked at the young man, barely more than a boy, and remembered herself at that age. She remembered how older men used to look at her back then; eyeing her, wanting her, and how it made her feel, both flattered and disgusted. She did like the fact that she was young and, in a sense, in control. If she wanted to, she could easily have slept with any of them; it was up to her. But as time went on and she slowly aged, the power that youth provided started to fade. And now things were different. She tried not to let Tyler know she wanted him, and she found herself feeling like one of those older men from her youth, wanting what they couldn't have. She vowed she would never use her position to push the issue, after all, she was an honorable woman. But still, she fantasized about what it would be like to have him. She was still a virile woman, one with needs, who was stuck on this yacht with a sexy young man she couldn't have. He would come out of the shower, loosely wrapped in a towel, and innocently walk around the cabin, oblivious to how his appearance might affect her. He meant no harm, but sometimes it was a torture to her. She wondered what would happen if she asked him to visit her cabin just once. The thought of it started a yearning within her. But she never did. She chose to suffer in silence.

"You going on shore with them tonight?" she asked Tyler.

"Yeah, if you don't mind," he replied.

"Probably a good idea," she said, sipping her iced tea. "Keep an eye on them."

"I will," Tyler replied

Tyler sat back, running through a mental list of the chores he needed to do on a daily basis, checking them off in his head. "I'd better go down to check the oil in the engines and the sea-strainers," he said, standing up. "You need anything?"

Seeing him in front of her, she thought of a task of her own she'd like to check off her list. "No, I'm good."

He turned and headed for the flybridge ladder and in an instant she was alone again, onboard and in command of a two-million-dollar yacht, looking at the soon-to-be-setting sun off the starboard beam and evaluating her life. She could clearly see the island from the bridge. Quite a few people were already on shore, setting up a bonfire and taking coolers onto the beach. Probably an hour of daylight was left. She decided to wait until just before sunset to wake the guests.

****

Being in the dinghy at night was a different experience from their earlier trips to the island. From *Dividends*, the trip looked like a short swim, but once in the boat, with darkness all around, it seemed like a long journey. Everyone was required to wear a life jacket at night. It was a company rule, and even though Harry felt it a bit emasculating, he understood the dangers of being out at night in the little boat. Tyler had a cooler onboard with contributions for the party from the ship's stores. Soon, they reached the shore, where he helped Beth off the boat, then turned his attentions to securing it by taking the anchor a distance up the beach and burying it in the sand. He then grabbed the cooler and, assisted by Harry, carried it up the beach to the roaring bonfire. A number of people were already at the party, and they warmly welcomed the three. A grill was covered with steaks, chicken, burgers, and hotdogs and a table holding side dishes. A CD player provided a variety of music. Couples sat around the fire on blankets, camp chairs, and loungers. Tyler placed their contributions on the table with the rest.

A middle-aged couple walked up and introduced themselves. The wife, who was obviously an outspoken extrovert, took Beth's hand, while her more conservative husband, drink in his hand, just smiled and let her do the talking. "Welcome. My name is Jenna. And you are?"

"Beth," she responded.

"Beth," Jenna repeated. "What a beautiful name. This is my husband, Steve," she said as she turned around and led Beth away.

Steve smiled and watched them go. Then he turned to Harry and extended his hand.

"Harry," Harry said, taking Steve's hand.

"Good to meet you, Harry," Steve said. He then motioned to the two women walking away.

"Forget it, Harry. She's gone for the night."

Harry, realizing that Beth would be occupied for the next few hours, turned his attention to his new friend. “So, Steve, what do you know?” he asked humorously.

“Absolutely nothing and I prove it on a daily basis.”

They walked over to the food and began to dig in.

Beth sat with Jenna and started to have, for lack of a better description, a slumber party. After they talked for a while, Jenna turned the conversation to Harry. She was sure the two were a couple, but was curious about the details.

Then they both noticed Tyler taking a burger from the grill and loading up a plate.

“Wow, who’s the beefcake?” Jenna asked, looking at his lean, muscular, young body silhouetted in the firelight.

“That’s Tyler,” Beth explained “I don’t get him.”

“Boy, I’d sure like to.”

“I don’t understand it, Jenna. He hasn’t so much as taken a second look at me since I met him. I love Harry—he’s the best thing that ever happened to me—but I’m used to getting those looks. You know what I mean?”

“Yeah, I know,” Jenna replied, the conversation barely registering as she undressed Tyler with her eyes.

“I walked around in my t-back and even had him put sunscreen on me, but he couldn’t wait to get back to fishing,” she said with obvious frustration. “I don’t get it.”

As Jenna watched, Tyler began talking to another handsome young man. She smiled, understanding Beth’s frustration, and said, “I think I see your problem,” motioning toward Tyler.

Just as Beth looked up, the young man put his hand in Tyler’s in an act of obvious affection.

Beth stared at him, speechless. “You’ve got to be kidding me,” she finally managed.

“What a waste,” Jenna said, staring through her glass.

"Well, that explains a lot," Beth said, feeling her self-confidence return. "No wonder he isn't interested."

They laughed together.

Harry and Steve sat and talked while eating. He watched Beth as she learned the truth about Tyler and laughed to himself, after which he let Steve in on the joke. They had a good chuckle over it.

"Just goes to show, you never can tell," Steve said.

"So, are you leaving in the morning?" Harry asked.

"If the wind is up, I will. If not, I'll probably hang around."

"What do you do, Steve?"

"These days, as little as possible," he replied, taking a sip of his bourbon and cola.

"Retired?"

"Last year. I still own the business, but my son is running it now. I realized that life is too short to do nothing but work. I worked hard all my life, and it's time to enjoy myself a little. I made quite a bit of money over the years, and the stock market has been good to me. I still have my health, my wife, and my freedom, so I decided to enjoy them while I can. You only have so much time. It's a treasure you shouldn't waste."

Harry sat quietly, absorbing Steve's words. It was the same advice Stan had given him, and they were both right. This was what life was about—living, not just preparing. He was going to live the time he had left like there was no tomorrow.

Chapter Ten

Maria watched the weather report on the satellite TV. She noted a system of bad weather forming to the northwest and moving toward them. It was going to get rough in a few hours, and there was no way to avoid it. She didn't want to be stuck in this relatively shallow water if they were to face a storm. Better to be in deeper water where grounding in the trough of high seas or being thrown up on a beach by high winds was less likely. They had some time, but they would have to get underway soon. She picked up the two-way radio to call Tyler.

"Tyler," the radio crackled. "Tyler, are you there?" Maria's voice called through the radio, now forgotten in the sand. "Tyler."

Tyler was with a friend from another boat, an old acquaintance he hadn't seen in quite some time. As they talked, the evening and *Dividends* drifted from his thoughts. They'd walked a long way down the beach together, and the light from the bonfire was lost in the darkness of the island night. They were in their own world until Tyler heard an extremely faint boom of thunder riding the wind from the northwest. There wasn't a cloud in the sky, the stars shone clear and bright, but Tyler knew what he'd heard. It snapped him back to reality, and he listened more closely. He heard Maria's voice on the radio and ran over to where he'd left it in the sand. "Tyler here," he replied.

"Tyler, we've got weather coming. Get them back on the boat and get back here."

"I'm on it," he replied as he and his friend hastened back to the bonfire.

Tyler found Harry and told him they had to get back to the boat. They collected Beth from her chatty new friend and headed to the shore, climbed into the skiff, and shoved off. With Harry and Beth on the skiff, they motored back as fast as they could on the now slightly choppy water.

Arriving at *Dividends*, Harry and Beth climbed onboard through the transom door, then Tyler brought the dinghy around to the port side where Maria had the crane cable extended. He hooked the bridle to it and centered his weight in the small boat. Maria hit the control to raise the dinghy out of the water. As it reached the bow rail, Tyler leaped onboard and began to control the skiff as Maria rotated it inboard and lowered it onto its deck-mounted chocks. The crane was disconnected and stowed, and Tyler set to work fastening down the dinghy and covering it up.

He was almost finished when Maria started the engines and called down, asking him to unlock the anchor chain. He ran to the bow and removed the lock so she could retrieve the anchor remotely from the bridge. Tyler noticed some sea grass caught on the anchor chain, which he manually removed to keep it from being pulled into the anchor locker. Once the chain was stowed and the anchor seated into the pulpit, he relocked the chain and headed into the cabin to make sure everything was secured and the hatches battened down for foul weather.

On the bridge, Maria was tuning the fifty-mile radar. At the edge of the screen, she could see the storm front begin its slow but deliberate march toward their position. She pushed the shifters forward, and *Dividends* began clawing its way out of the shallow water and toward the safety of the open sea.

Harry and Beth went below and settled into the salon.

Tyler brought a couple of life jackets to them. "We're going to get into some weather, so if you come out on deck, be sure to put these on."

He took two more up to the bridge for himself and Maria.

Looking out over the bow, they stared into a dark abyss. It was as though the world ceased to exist ahead of them. After reaching deeper water and a safe distance from the island, Maria turned northeast to try to skirt the storm. If it turned to the south, it was possible they would miss most of it; if it turned to the east, it would hit them right on. They watched the radar, the only way to see as they progressed through the darkness. Blips on the screen indicated other boats following their example. Some headed south, obviously betting the storm would turn to the east. It would be a rough night for some of them and only time would tell which.

****

Harry and Beth were in their cabin watching the satellite TV when they heard a knock on the door. Opening the door, Beth found Tyler wearing a life jacket and carrying the life jackets he'd given them in the salon.

"I need you to put these on," Tyler said calmly.

"What's wrong?" Beth asked. "Are we sinking?"

"No, we're fine, but the storm has turned to the east and we're going to be in the middle of it. Company rules require that guests wear life jackets if we encounter a storm."

They donned the bulky orange vests, cinching them up, and then followed Tyler to the flybridge.

The sea was still relatively calm, but they could feel the high pressure and humidity in the air as they motored toward the storm. Occasional lightning strikes showed the rough conditions ahead. One look at the radar showed the distance to the weather front which was now only ten miles away and closing fast.

"Can't we turn around and try to outrun it?" Harry asked.

"No," Maria replied. "It's moving too fast. If we try to outrun it, it would overtake us and we could be in it for days. We'll go right through it and come out on the other side, keeping our bow into the wind and waves. It's the safest course of action. Don't worry; *Dividends* can handle it."

Harry wasn't worried. He thought it was exciting. But Beth was scared and clung to Harry for dear life. She'd never been through anything like this. The storm was on them in what seemed like minutes. The cold front hit, and the four of them found themselves holding on as the yacht was tossed up and down, cresting the peak of each wave and falling into the troughs in between. Maria used the engines to keep the bow as high as possible, but it was no use. After cresting each wave, the bow plunged into the next and disappeared, plowing through the dark water, deeper and deeper as the waves got higher and closer together. That's when they began to hear a slamming, crashing noise with each wave, but couldn't see what was wrong.

Tyler held onto the railing around the front of the flybridge and looked through the partially opened zipper in the enclosure as they plowed through the next wave. That's when he saw it.

"Oh, my God!" Tyler exclaimed as he turned to Maria. "The dinghy is loose!"

In his hurry to release the anchor chain, he'd never secured the stern of the dinghy, and it was slamming down on the chocks with each wave. "If you can keep her steady, I'll get it locked down," he yelled.

"He'll be washed overboard!" Harry protested.

"No, I'll be OK. But if that dinghy comes loose and crashes through the front of the salon, we could go down."

Maria slowed the engines to minimize the water coming over the bow, and Tyler raced up the port side and onto the front deck. As he reached the dinghy, a wave broke over the bow, knocking him off his feet and pushing him toward the edge of the deck. He reached up and caught the leg of the chock, which stopped him from being swept overboard. At the same time, the stern of the dinghy was swept out of the chock and crashed down on the deck. Tyler sprung to his feet and grabbed the transom of the dinghy, trying to lift it back into the chock. He pulled and strained, but couldn't get secured. Harry raced down the ladder and worked his way to the bow to help. Another wave broke over the bow, knocking them both off their feet, but their grip on the stern of the skiff kept them safe. They got to their feet and, together, lifted the dinghy into the chock. Tyler rushed to lock it down securely, and they started making their way back on the starboard side. That's when it hit.

Up on the bridge, Maria had control of the boat and began to throttle up again as the men worked their way back. She turned slightly to starboard to quarter the waves and protect them from being washed overboard. Beth was hanging on the starboard side of the bridge as she watched the men prepare to enter the cockpit. Then they felt the boat list severely to the left and get thrown violently to the right as a rogue wave slammed into the port side. Maria, caught off guard, was thrown past Beth and over the side. Her legs caught the bulkhead, and she was cart-wheeling in the air as she hit the surf. Beth stood in shock as she watched their captain, the one they counted on with their very lives, fly helplessly through the air and into rough water.

Tyler cleared the flybridge ladder and took the helm. He caught a glimpse of Maria hitting the surf and had to get to her. By the time he got from the side of the cabin to the helm, *Dividends* had crossed a lot of water with no one at the helm. At sea, there are no points of reference other than electronics. Tyler timed the waves and spun the wheel, bringing the boat around, and then marked the position on the GPS. Maria was lost, and he intended to find her.

"Grab the life ring on the rail and be ready to throw it to her," he shouted to Harry.

Harry grabbed the ring and prepared himself.

Tyler looked into the surf for a tiny light. Each of the life jackets had a light that activated when it hit the water. It was Maria's only hope. They looked into the darkness for what seemed like an eternity; waves crested and fell in the darkness. Lightning flashes temporarily gave a daylight view of the rough sea, but hampered their night vision. They turned off all the lights on the boat in an effort to make it easier to spot the life jacket's light, but there was no sign. Tyler went past where he thought she might be and turned again, putting the boat back on their original course. Then he returned to the marked position to begin an organized search. She was his captain, she was like a mother to him, she was his best friend, and he couldn't leave her. Beth started to cry.

Chapter Eleven

Maria floated alone in the dark. She'd been knocked unconscious on impact with the water. When she regained consciousness, it took her a few minutes to get her bearings and understand what had happened. She began turning in circles, looking for the boat. The light on her lifejacket, although small, was bright as a searchlight in the blackness. She was lifted and lowered with each wave, and she tried to look in all directions on each peak. She thought of Tyler and how her life was now in his hands. She wondered if he was thrown overboard, too. If that was the case, she was doomed.

Dividends was nowhere in sight. "Maybe she went down," she spoke aloud.

How bad could that wave have been? She thought of how she'd always wanted Tyler, and how she'd never tried to be with him. She regretted it now. She wondered if this was the end. Would she drown? Would she be taken by a predator? Would she die of exposure? Still looking for the boat, she began to panic, followed by despair.

****

Hours passed, the storm subsided, and the waters calmed. Harry went up on the bow and to the end of the pulpit to look for the light. Tyler returned to the point he figured was closest to where Maria had fallen overboard and circled in a spiral pattern, looking for her. He knew she would be drawn with the current, but he kept to his pattern so as not to leave any area unsearched. He knew if she survived the fall, with the life jacket, she would be on the surface. His only fear was that the sun would come up and eliminate any chance of seeing the tiny light. They were on their way down current, the most likely direction, as a slight hint of the sunrise appeared in the east. Tyler began to lose hope.

"There she is!" Harry screamed, pointing to a tiny light about one thousand yards off the bow, defiant in the night.

Tyler slammed the throttles forward and locked his eyes on the spot. *Dividends* lurched forward and climbed up on plane. He saw the light, but that didn't mean she was OK. He had to get to her. He had to discipline himself to slow the boat as he approached so as not to pass by her. Maria was facing the other direction.

She was unconscious again, floating limply in the now-gentle waves. Tyler reversed the engines, stopping the boat. He climbed to the side of the flybridge and dove off to get to her. Harry threw the life ring to them. Tyler reached her and grabbed the handle on the back of her life jacket. With two strokes, he reached the life ring. Harry pulled both to the transom and helped them onboard.

Maria was groggy but responsive. Beth took charge and escorted their battered captain to the cabin where she stayed to look after her.

Tyler shifted the transmissions forward and *Dividends* responded at a slow crawl. He turned northwest and set the autopilot. The storm was off to the east and that direction would take them toward Florida. Leaving Harry on the bridge, Tyler set to work getting the boat ship shape again.

"You realize you're a hero," Harry said to Tyler, who was stowing the life ring.

"I'm not a hero," he said. "It's my job. Can you watch things for me? I want to check on her."

"Sure," Harry replied, heading for the bridge.

Tyler found Beth waiting outside the door to the master cabin's shower. Maria was under the hot water, trying to return her body temperature to normal. Beth looked at Tyler and knew he wanted to be alone with his captain and friend. She handed him the bathrobe she was holding for Maria and left the cabin.

"Are you all right?" Tyler asked through the closed door.

The water shut off, and she replied, "Yes."

The door opened, and Tyler handed in the robe.

"Thank you," Maria said.

A moment later, she came out wearing the robe and a towel around her head. "Tyler, you saved my life. Thank you. I mean it."

"How do you feel?" he asked.

"Fortunate. I can't believe you found me," she said.

"You taught me."

"How long was I out there?"

"Hours," he said. "I'm not sure how many. By the time I was able to get to the bridge and take the helm, you were gone. We circled until we found you."

She stretched her neck. "The last thing I remember is getting thrown off the bridge, then waking up alone."

"You need anything?"

She was overcome by what had happened to her. She thought about how she'd felt, floating, alone, and how she wished she'd been with Tyler just once. She stared at him without a word for a long minute, and then she said, "Yes." She was about to tell him that she needed him, but instead she replied, "Rest. Take command of the boat and get us to port. I know I'm asking you a lot after last night, but I need some sleep. Can you handle that for me?"

"No problem," Tyler responded. "Get some sleep, I'll keep things slow and calm, and I'll check on you in a few hours."

"Thank you," she said as she put her arms around him, giving him a hug.

Tyler left her there to get some rest and headed back to the bridge. He found Harry at the helm of *Dividend*, still in neutral and engines at idle. When he got close, Harry started to back away from the controls.

"No, you look good there, Harry," Tyler told him. "Shift those levers forward."

Harry pushed the transmission shifters that Tyler pointed to and the boat moved forward slowly. Tyler looked at the screen on the GPS and determined the course that would take them back to their home port. He pointed to the compass and told Harry to turn the boat until the lubber lines matched up with the proper heading. Tyler then added a little throttle until the engines were synchronized and sat back in the second seat, leaving Harry to pilot the boat under his supervision.

"How's Maria?" Harry asked.

"She'll be ok," Tyler said. "She just needs some rest."

They cruised for the next few hours at a slow pace. The storm was over, so they didn't have any reason to hurry back to port. Beth prepared some sandwiches for them and took one to Maria. She found her awake in the cabin.

Maria took the sandwich and asked, "Is everything going ok up there?"

"Yeah, Tyler is showing Harry how to drive the boat."

"That's great. Would you ask Tyler to come down here please?"

"Sure," Beth replied. "I'll send him right down." Beth left the cabin and, arriving back on the bridge, delivered the message.

Tyler left *Dividends* in Harry's hands and hurried down to the cabin. He knocked on the door and Maria invited him in. Maria was sitting on the edge of the bed, wearing the bathrobe that he'd handed her. He came in leaving the door open.

"Close the door," she said.

Tyler turned around and secured the door as he asked, "Is there something I can do for you?"

"Yes," she said, dropping the bathrobe. "There is something I need."

Tyler turned back around to face her just as the bathrobe hit the floor. He looked at her beautiful naked body and didn't know what to do. She moved toward him and around him, pinning him against the bed. She pulled the towel from her head and let her silky, jet black hair spill out. Tyler was gay, but he was aroused by her aggressive behavior. He'd never thought of her this way. She removed his shorts and pushed him back onto the bed, climbing on top of him. Tyler didn't resist.

Maria knew she'd regret this later and that things would never be the same between them, but she didn't care. She knew what she wanted—that strong, young, athletic body. He might hate her tomorrow, but he was hers for now, and it was too late to stop. She began to make love to the young man she'd dreamed about. She was a woman in need, in need of the attention of a strong young man, and Tyler cooperated.

She had fantasized about this moment. Now it was finally going to happen. He put his arms around her and they made love together.

****

Beth was on the flybridge with Harry, watching him run the boat. This was his first time at the helm of a boat. Although, on autopilot, a boat this large runs itself. Still, Harry felt as if he was in command.

The sun was well above the horizon and the weather had cleared drastically.

Beth looked at him standing at the helm. His rugged looks made him appear right at home at the wheel.

"How's she doing?" he asked her.

"She got some sleep," Beth replied. "She's OK."

"You OK?"

"Yeah, I was scared, though. I can still see her flying over the side, right in front of me. It was like everything was in slow motion, but there was nothing I could do."

"She was lucky. She could have been lost at sea," Harry said.

Tyler came back up to the bridge and took command of the helm.

"Thanks, Harry," he said, taking the wheel. Tyler programmed the autopilot to take them back to Fort Lauderdale, a two-day journey at their slow pace, so he pushed the throttles forward and took the boat up to top cruising speed.

"Maria OK?" Harry asked.

"Yeah. She'll be OK," Tyler replied.

Harry and Beth both noticed that there was something on his mind. They looked at each other and didn't ask any more questions.

****

By the time they approached port, Maria had once again taken control of *Dividends*. She didn't mention the ordeal, but there was something going on between her and Tyler. They did their jobs, but as if they were strangers. The laughter and camaraderie they'd shared was gone; there was no unnecessary communication between them. They got the boat back to port and into the slip. As they shut down, Maria called Tyler to the bridge.

"I'm sorry, Tyler," she said, searching for the right words. "I don't know what else to say."

"There isn't much to say. I never looked at you that way. How can anything ever be the same?"

"It can't."

"So I guess I'm going to lose my job now."

"No," she said. "I am."

"I don't understand," he said. "You're the captain."

"I'm resigning as captain."

"What about me? If you leave, they'll hire a new captain, and it's up to the new captain to hire the crew."

"Nobody knows or loves this boat the way you do, Tyler. I'll ask that they keep you on. Who knows, maybe you'll be the next skipper."

"I doubt that," he said, feeling like his world was coming to an end.

"I just can't do it anymore," she said. "Do you hate me?"

"Of course not," he replied. "I just wish it could go back to the way it was."

"That wouldn't work for me," Maria said. "I'm ready for a change in my life. I'm getting older and want to do new things. I want to have a relationship, a home, maybe kids, and that's impossible when I'm gone for weeks at a time."

"I understand. So it's not about what happened yesterday morning?" Tyler asked.

"No. This has been coming on for a while. What happened yesterday morning was something that I've wanted to happen for a long time and something that I'll always cherish, but my decision to leave the boat was made before that," she explained. "No hard feelings?"

After a long pause, "No hard feelings," he managed.

****

Tyler took Harry and Beth's bags to his truck before leaving for the airport. He cleared the seat and held the door for them, but he was definitely preoccupied. Harry felt these last couple of weeks had made them friends rather than acquaintances, so it wouldn't be out of line to ask what was wrong.

"What is it, Tyler?" he asked.

"Nothing, Harry," Tyler replied.

"What is it, Tyler?" he asked again.

Tyler stopped, took a breath, and confided in his new friend. "Maria is resigning as captain," he said quietly, sitting sideways in the truck. "That means my days on the boat are numbered. This boat and this job are all I have."

"Why is she resigning? Is she scared after what happened?"

"No, I don't think so," Tyler said. "I've never known her to be scared of anything."

"What is it then?"

"She's tired of being on the water all the time. She wants to move on."

"Don't worry, Tyler," Harry said. "Things will work out. You're a great first mate. You'll do well."

"We'll see," he replied half-heartedly. "We should get going."

Before leaving, they ran through their checklist to be sure they hadn't forgotten anything.

"Passports?"

"Check."

"Luggage?"

"Check."

"Travelers checks?"

"Check."

Finally, the list was exhausted, and Tyler whisked them away to the nightmare that was the airport. They said goodbye to Tyler and, after wading through the confusion of security checkpoints, signs, and directions to the correct terminal, they were on their way at last.

Chapter Twelve

Arriving in the Caymans, they went directly to the company condo and settled in.

It was a beautiful place; the company had spared no expense. Strangely, it was one of the things on Harry's list of assets to sell in his plan to increase company growth. He wondered how many executives he'd pissed off with that one. He thought it was just an expense on a balance sheet, but he realized it was very different when you were standing in the living room.

Beth went from room to room, taking it all in. She'd never experienced anything like this. First, the beautiful yacht and the trip to a secluded island. Now, the comfort of the condo and restaurants accompanied by beautiful beaches. Usually her vacations were weekend excursions to a cheap motel with the boyfriend of the month, near some attraction she didn't much care about. But here she was, standing in paradise—again. What did she want to do first? What would any woman want to do first in an island paradise?

"Let's take a walk on the beach!" she said to Harry.

"You got it," Harry replied, although tired but not wanting to spoil her mood.

They changed their clothes and headed out the door. The elevator opened to the smell of coconut oil and the sounds of families heading for the beach. One of the larger families struggled with a pile of beach towels, slippery bottles of tanning oil, and an excess of cameras and coolers. All were wearing big floppy straw hats, unflattering bathing suits, and—the badge of a tourist—a big smear of white sunscreen on their noses. The parents herded their hyperactive children through the lobby toward the beach.

Harry and Beth smiled at each other and she giggled a little while watching the tourist family in their plight. Beth was glued to Harry's arm as they walked through the lobby. They went out into the afternoon sun and felt its warmth engulf them. The sounds of seagulls, the feel and scent of the sea air seemed to wash away the stress and confusion of the day. The sand under their feet was hot, but not too hot to walk barefoot. They enjoyed the feel of it between their toes.

Trying to avoid the scantily clad beachgoers and Frisbee-throwing teenagers near the condo, they headed toward a less populated area. The sounds of the crowd faded, replaced by the gentle sounds of waves crashing on the shore. Even the seagulls left them alone, staying near the tourists with food that they could try to steal.

"You relaxed?" Harry asked.

"This is beautiful, baby. Thank you for bringing me here," she replied.

"It wouldn't be without you."

Beth sighed. She squeezed him tightly and said the words neither had yet said to each other—those three powerful words that change things forever.

"I love you."

"I love you, too," Harry said, turning to face her and putting his arms around her.

That was it. Nothing would ever be the same again. They both felt it; they both knew it. The barrier was broken. They'd been lovers before, not much more than good friends with benefits, but now they were in love. Harry looked at Beth in a whole new light. It was as if they had never existed apart. He couldn't imagine life without her; he wanted her to spend her life with him. He'd made up his mind that, by the end of the trip, he was going to make it permanent.

Beth felt the power of the moment as well. She didn't say those words lightly. She loved him. No one had ever treated her like Harry did. She kept looking for a chink in his armor but hadn't found any. There was the age difference, but that comforted her. He was smart and strong, and his rugged good looks were a bonus. She felt safe in his arms, important in his life, and captivated in his bed.

Feeling the sun's effect on their relatively unprotected skin, they cut their walk short and headed back to the protection of the condo. Right behind the condo, facing the beach, was a little oasis and bar. Scattered palm trees and beach cabanas provided shelter and a welcome break from the sun. Guests with tropical drinks and dark tans meandered, lounging in the shelters, enjoying the world between the heat of the beach and the solitude of their condos.

Harry bought drinks, and they relaxed in lounge chairs under a cabana facing the water. The sound of the surf was soothing, and the tropical music played by an island band accentuated it.

Sipping his drink, Harry broke the quiet, saying, "Hot sun, cool drink, great view…it doesn't get any better than this!"

"Word!" Beth replied.

"Word?" Harry asked, humorously acknowledging the age difference between them.

"Word," she said again, staring at him as if to say "duh."

They sipped their drinks in silence. Then, after a moment, Harry let out a long slow breath, slowly saying, "Word."

Beth smiled and relaxed, enjoying his attempt to be a part of her generation. She was having a great time. Looking over at the man who made it all possible, she thought back to the life she knew before they met, which was little more than an existence. It seemed like a chapter had ended and a new one had begun, a point in time in which all her dreams could come true. She wasn't a gold digger; she really loved Harry. But it didn't hurt that he was a man of means. She didn't know how much money he had, and she didn't care. It hadn't spoiled him. She'd met men who let money go to their heads, the kind of men who thought money gave them the right to be pigs and to treat girls like her as possessions rather than people. Harry wasn't like that at all. He acted as though he didn't have any money. He always treated her like a lady.

Beth snapped back to reality with the sound of Harry's voice. "What're you thinkin' about, baby?"

She blinked and grinned, realizing he was focused on her and she'd been a million miles away.

"Nothin'. I just zoned out."

"Everything OK?"

"Great. I'm just taking it all in."

****

Morning came, and Harry awoke cuddled around Beth. The only sound in the condo was her sleepy breathing. The room was dark and cool, but light crept in around the heavy drapes covering the balcony doors. He slid out of bed quietly and made his way to the kitchen to start the coffee. It wasn't until the coffee was ready that Beth got up. Harry, with cup in hand, watched Beth as she stirred and yawned. She rolled over to Harry's side of the bed only to find him missing. She quickly wiped the sleep from her eyes and looked around. Seeing Harry in the kitchen area, she smiled.

"Got one of those for me?" she asked.

Harry took the cup he'd already poured for her to the bed. She took it gratefully, and after a careful sip, sighed with pleasure.

"Mmmm, thank you, baby," she said, setting the cup on the nightstand. Then she made her way to the bathroom.

Harry watched her firm naked body walking slowly and seductively away from him. He couldn't believe how lucky he was that this beautiful woman was with him. He was going to suggest they go out to breakfast, but soon realized Beth had a suggestion of her own.

She emerged from the bathroom and walked back to the bed where Harry was waiting for her.

She slid in next to him and began to kiss him passionately.

Harry's body agreed with her plan and soon they found themselves clinging together in the throes of passion. Soft light from the kitchen gently illuminated them as they made love.

Afterwards, Harry opened the heavy drapes to reveal the amazing view, crawled back into bed, and cuddled up behind Beth, pulling her close, holding her tightly. Beth finally broke the silence.

"How come you never got married, Harry?" she asked.

Harry took a few moments before responding, "Didn't we cover this ground?"

"You said you'd never been married, you didn't say why."

"It's kind of a long story."

"We have all day."

"You really want to know?"

"Yeah. You're such a great guy. I just wondered why you're still on the market."

"Am I still on the market?"

She chuckled lightly and nudged him. "Come on, you know what I mean."

Harry thought about it. He knew the answer. He thought of the long years of struggle, the feelings that enough was never enough, the drive for money and power that always seemed just out of reach. He thought of all the late nights, weekends, and vacations he'd missed working to beat deadlines, pushing toward the undefined goal he hoped to reach so his life could begin. Did he really want to pile all that on her? Would that taint how she saw him? And what difference would it make in their relationship? He decided to take the easy way out.

"I just never met the right girl," he replied.

She squeezed the arms surrounding her as they spooned together, watching seagulls fly by the window in the early morning light. That was the answer she wanted, and she was fulfilled.

But his answer didn't sit right with him, and he regretted saying it. It wasn't exactly a lie. He hadn't met the right girl before, but it wasn't because they weren't out there. He hadn't been looking. He wasn't ready to look for a wife. It was ironic. The quest for money and power brought him to the reality that the quest itself had been consuming his life. Had it not been for Stan, he might never have raised his head to look around and see the world. He'd asked Harry, "What makes you, well, you?" Had it not been for that inquiry, Harry might not have awakened until it was too late. He might never have met Beth. But now he was awake. He felt he finally knew the answer to Stan's question, and he felt ready to join the upper ranks of the corporate world.

They donned their tourist garb and left the condo well before noon, heading out to look for a quaint little spot for a much-needed brunch. Finding a small restaurant down the street, they settled in a booth.

The place was decorated in an island theme, comfortable and inviting. The waiter took their orders and they sat back to wait.

Beth browsed through some tourist brochures she'd found in a display at the entrance to the deli.

"What you got there, baby?" Harry asked.

"I'm just deciding what kind of island adventure you're going to take me on today," she replied, with a tone of false command.

"Oh, it's like that, is it?" he retorted with a smile, picking up his drink.

The waiter noticed the scene and piped in. "You two should go to Hell," he said to them with a straight face.

Harry looked at the waiter, shocked. "What did you say?"

The waiter replied, "I said you two should go to Hell." This time the waiter smiled and pointed at one of the brochures lying on the table. "It's a popular spot for tourists."

Beth was smiling and trying not to laugh. Harry, about to make an example of the waiter, got the joke and smiled himself.

"Sorry, guys. I couldn't resist. That's one of my favorite jokes," the waiter said as he walked away smiling.

Beth opened the brochure the waiter had pointed to, and sure enough, there it was. "Hell, Grand Cayman. You want to check this out?" she asked. "There's even a post office there where we can send postcards from Hell."

"Sure, if you want to," Harry said. "After that, I want to find a place to take dive lessons."

"Awesome," she replied.

After lunch, they got a taxi and Beth commanded, "Take us straight to Hell."

The driver knew exactly what she was talking about, and they were off.

Hell was surprisingly crowded, but not so badly they couldn't make their way onto the boardwalk to see the main attraction. There they found the million-year-old rock formations that gave the area its name. They looked like a small mountain range. Tourists were not allowed to walk among them, but they could see them perfectly from the two boardwalks constructed for the purpose.

Snapping pictures and enjoying the day, the couple made their way to a post office painted a deep, fire-engine red. There they addressed postcards, sending them to friends and co-workers at home. They even sent them to each other. They also visited a multitude of souvenir shops, and with bags in hand, they were on their way back.

They hailed a cab and asked the cab driver where they could get dive lessons near the condo. The driver recommended a place and dropped them at André's Dive Shop, which was conveniently just a short walk from the condo. There they met André, the dive master, instructor, and owner of the shop. André was a native islander with a somewhat exaggerated island accent. He was a strongly built man, about forty years old, and his rugged appearance oozed confidence.

André told Harry he didn't have a class scheduled, but after Harry expressed interest in purchasing complete sets of equipment for the two of them, the shop owner offered them private lessons. They agreed and were sent home with some books and info they could look over. Their classes would start the next day, take a few days to complete, and consist of both pool and open water dives. They went back to the condo and looked over the dive gear they had purchased.

Harry bought matching gear for both of them, his in blue and hers in pink. It had taken some time to fit everything, but it was well worth it. The masks, booties, fins, weight belts, buoyancy control devices, and gloves all fit perfectly. Harry looked over the equipment. He was excited about the classes. The two of them poured over the books they were given and tried to get a handle on this new world they had only seen on television. Tomorrow, they would be in that world, and they wanted to be ready.

The next morning, they went to the dive shop with all their gear. André led them to a makeshift classroom set up for twenty students, and they got right to work. The emptiness of the large room made Harry feel a little like he was back in school and had to stay for detention, but that soon passed as he became engrossed in dive tables, nitrogen narcosis, and breathing techniques.

There was a lot of information to absorb, and André went over it again and again until he was sure they had each lesson down pat. They broke for lunch, and when they returned it was more of the same. That afternoon, André told them it was time to suit up for some in-water training in the pool.

"Where do we go for that?" Harry asked, not having seen a pool on the property.

"In the next room," André replied, and led them to a fairly large, deep indoor pool that took up half the small building. They then went to dressing rooms to put on their bathing suits.

Beth emerged wearing the black suit she'd bought for the trip. Her usually flowing hair, now bundled up in a ponytail, looked somewhat out of place with the sexy suit.

André, who had seen thousands of women walk out of those dressing room doors, remained professional, showing no sign that he even noticed her beautiful body. Instead, he led the couple to the tank rack, asking them each to select a tank and carry it to the prep area. He led them through the procedure of assembling the tank, BC, and regulator set in preparation for their first dive.

André then asked, "What do we do if we get into trouble?"

Both Beth and Harry answered what they'd been taught only hours earlier. "Breathe."

They stood up and helped each other with the gear as they were taught, checking and rechecking each other's equipment, then they stepped off into the pool, first Beth, then Harry, and finally André.

Harry felt a rush as he realized that he was breathing underwater. It seemed surreal. He'd spent the entire morning learning about it, but until he hit the water, it didn't click. He looked at Beth, who was also trying to get used to the feeling.

Beth looked funny with the mask pressed tightly against her face and the huge regulator in her mouth. Her eyes were wide open and she appeared to be on the edge of panic, but she soon became accustomed to breathing underwater and began swimming around the pool.

They had totally forgotten about André, who was watching them from a distance. He knew that there was no sense trying to teach them anything now. He had seen it with virtually everyone he had taught. For the first five minutes or so, new divers had to get the strangeness out of their systems, so he did what he always did—watched and waited until they got the hang of it. He loved it. Seeing new divers swimming around for the first time was always rewarding for him. He liked teaching them, and he felt a real sense of accomplishment when they passed the tests and became certified divers.

When the pair got comfortable in their new environment, they looked around for André. That was his cue to get to work. He swam over to them, and they began to work on the drills they'd learned in the classroom: emergency ascents, buddy breathing, removing and replacing gear underwater, and clearing their masks. Each went like clockwork.

****

André was a great instructor and by the end of the second day, they were ready for their open-water dive.

"OK, guys," André began at the end of the final lesson. "We have an open-water dive tomorrow. It's a group dive with some graduating students as well as some veteran divers. All the tanks will be onboard, so just bring your gear and be at the dock at seven a.m. sharp. At the end of the dive, you will be certified."

Harry and Beth looked at each other, smiling with a sense of pride.

"We'll be there," Harry responded.

Beth nodded in agreement.

They gathered their belongings and headed back to the condo. The day of lessons left them exhausted, Harry more so than Beth. He attributed it to age and relaxed on the balcony the rest of the day.

They were up at the crack of dawn the next morning. A hurried breakfast was followed by a mad dash out the door with their dive gear and a cooler of lunch, water, and juices. Arriving at the dock, they met André, who boarded them and watched as they did a gear check before leaving the dock. It wasn't until they'd cleared the outer marker of the harbor that Harry realized he'd forgotten his camera. He'd read all the directions, loaded it in its clear waterproof case, and left it on the dresser. There was no turning back now.

"Damn it!" he muttered.

"What's wrong?" Beth asked.

"The camera," he said, frustrated.

"You forgot it?"

"Of course."

"Don't worry about it. We'll have lots of time to take pictures. Let's just have fun."

The boat arrived at the dive site and tied off to a buoy that was permanently attached to the wreck. That was when the motion, the sound of the water, and the smell of the diesel engine began getting to some of the divers. The signs of seasickness were apparent on their faces.

Harry and Beth listened closely as André went over the safety rules. This was their first open-water dive, and they were more than a little nervous. Trying to take it all in, they were both excited and apprehensive.

Holding up his right hand, André said, "Let me see your hand if this be your first time."

Harry and Beth both felt relieved to see more than half the divers' hands go up. Harry thought that if there were this many "first timers," they must be used to looking out for them. After all, with this many new divers on every trip, the news would be flooded with reports of lost or "bent" divers if it were a problem.

André knew how to play up his native islander status. His island accent seemed natural, and he loved hamming it up for the tourists. "We be staying together on this dive. The current is not too strong, but it be there all the same. We don't be wanting to spend the rest of the day looking for them what get separated. After a long day on de water, I want to get to a cold beer, a warm woman, and good times on the island, not sitting in de police station filling out paperwork," André joked.

Everyone laughed as André started going through the needed steps to get them ready. This was a beginning-to-intermediate dive and it was a relatively small crowd, but there was always inherent danger when underwater, so André always ended his speech on a serious note. "If something goes wrong, what do we do?"

The entire group responded, in unison, "Breathe."

"Good," André replied with a smile. "Keep one eye on your buddy, one eye on your air pressure, one eye on your depth, and don't forget to use one eye to look at the beautiful fishes and things you might see down there. And if you don't know what it is, what do we do?"

"Don't touch it!"

"Good. Who has questions?" Seeing there were none, André motioned for everyone to stand up.

"OK, let's get going."

Harry had been feeling a little seasick, and it hit harder as he stood up in his dive gear, but the feeling vanished as he hit the water. His nerves were challenged by the new experience, but he focused on what he'd learned in the classes. His forgotten camera now seemed like a blessing—he could focus on the dive undistracted. There would be other dives and lots of opportunities for pictures.

Beth took to diving like a duck to water; she looked like she was having the time of her life. The other men on the boat, who'd been stealing looks at her during the entire ride, paused to watch her jump into the water with perfect form. She submerged, surfacing next to Harry with her hand above her head as she'd been taught.

Breathing through his snorkel, while waiting for the rest of the group to enter the water, Harry felt a little claustrophobic. He couldn't wait to get on with the dive. It was a relief when André got things started.

André stood at the end of the platform and asked, "Is everybody ready?" Seeing them pointing at the top of their heads—the universal diver's signal for 'OK'—he said, "Switch to your regulators and deflate your BCs." Then, seeing everyone had done so, André put his hand in front of his face, holding his regulator and mask, and jumped in himself.

He was a good dive master and had never had an injured diver. He watched each student, hovering above the group, ready to pounce on the first sign of trouble. They were diving on the wreck of a fishing boat in sixty-five feet of water. It was a good dive for first-timers, and with one focal point, the group had a tendency to stay together.

Harry watched the wreck appear through the haze. It was like something from another world. It looked out of place. He saw it get larger and larger and then realized that he'd forgotten a critical part of his training, inflating his BC. As he descended on the wreck, the pressure compressed the air in the BC, causing him to descend faster and faster. *Control your descent,* he thought in a panic. He reached for the low-pressure inflator on his BC and started applying air at the last second. But it was too late. He plowed into the wreck with a thud.

He wasn't hurt, but the danger wasn't over. He'd overinflated the BC and was starting to dart to the surface. He felt himself being jerked around by the straps on his BC and was surprised to see André, who immediately took Harry's hand off the inflator and dumped about half the air Harry had pumped into it. This arrested his ascent and stabilized his buoyancy. Harry hadn't realized he was in danger until that moment, but looking down, he realized he'd floated halfway back to the surface.

André, still holding Harry by the shoulder straps on his BC, got his attention and held a thumb up as if to ask, "Are you OK?" Harry replied with the same gesture and was released. He then descended slowly, controlling the air in his BC and paying attention to the other lessons he'd learned until he reached the wreck again. When he reached Beth, who'd been waiting patiently on the bottom, they circled the wreck as though nothing had happened.

The water was clear and cool, and they felt as though they were flying as they cruised around the wreck. Harry had all but forgotten about the embarrassment of his descent. The other divers, André, and even the wreck itself had somehow faded into the background. Now it was just Harry and Beth, flying along like birds, kicking and gliding, enjoying the experience.

When circling the wreck, Harry wished he had his camera. He wanted this moment preserved in a photo. He vowed to himself that he wouldn't forget it the next time. They marveled at the brilliant colors of everything there. The coral, the fish, the crustaceans, all displaying vivid hues that seemed so wasted in a world most people would never see.

Harry noticed something interesting. He saw that some of the small fish that had made the makeshift reef home were in pairs, traveling side by side. They seemed to have no direction—they turned one way, then changed course and swim the other, for reasons only they knew, but always together, sharing a harmonious dance through life. They didn't squabble or try to outdo the other; they enjoyed each other's company. The orange-and-white clownfish, the beautiful yellow-and-violet queen angelfish, and the royal blue tang all moved together with life partners, their brilliant colors a contrast against the background like ornaments on a Christmas tree.

What a lesson for human life, Harry thought to himself.

There were the others on the reef—the loners, the predators. They spent time cruising around, feeding on the other fish. They had a mean streak that was obvious on their sinister faces. Armed with the teeth, the strength, the speed, and the attitude, they prowled the structure for their next meal. Competing for their place in the food chain, they were the carnivores, eating those smaller, while trying not to be eaten by those larger and faster. The predators lived a lonely life, constantly struggling through their existence. They swam with purpose, constantly on the prowl for their next meal, oblivious to the tranquil world that was all around them.

Harry couldn't help but equate the behavior of the fish with that of humans. He'd spent his life as a predator, chewing up the lower-downs while trying not to be eaten by the higher-ups. He was the one swimming through life solo, racing through the world of business. Others, like his boss's secretary Heather, cruised through life with a soul mate, walking side by side, changing course together, having children, holding hands, and enjoying the euphoria of life together.

It was at that moment Harry had an epiphany. *That's what life is all about. It isn't the destination that's important. It is the journey. It is what we do with our time, the way we affect the lives of those we come in contact with that is important.* He was going to change the way he looked at life. He'd already started with Beth in his life. He was definitely going shopping for a ring.

"Bang, bang, bang."

The metallic sound of André tapping his dive knife on the side of his tank interrupted the quiet. The sound snapped Harry, as well as the rest of the divers, back to reality. André was pointing at his watch with the shiny blade, signifying it was time to leave this world behind.

Harry and Beth faced each other and kicked slowly upward, while gradually releasing air from their BCs to control their ascent. They kept their buoyancy neutral until they reached one of the safety lines hanging from the boat. They hung on for the minimum five minutes to make sure they'd expelled enough nitrogen from their blood to avoid an embolism. Then they made their way to the dive ladder.

Back onboard, the first mate, the captain, and André each did a headcount, making sure that no one was missing. The line to the anchor buoy was retrieved, and they were on their way.

Harry couldn't believe how tired he was, and he could see he wasn't the only one. The dive had taken a toll on all of them. The effects of breathing compressed air at depth causes extreme drowsiness when divers return to the surface.

"You all look like you could sleep for a week," André said, with a hint of humor. "Don't worry, it be normal. 'Tis the effect from the pressure and from the extra nitrogen in your blood. You will sleep like babies tonight."

André then went up to Harry and asked, "You OK?"

Harry noticed that André's voice was not only quiet, it was missing his usual strong island accent.

"Yeah, I'm OK," Harry replied. "Sorry about that."

"Don't worry about it. I'm just glad I got to you before you bobbed up like a cork."

"Yeah, me too."

Harry was embarrassed that it was brought up again, but he was relieved to see that none of the other divers paid any attention.

André then handed them their dive cards. "Congrats, guys. You are certified divers." He turned away to let them eat the lunch Beth was taking out of the cooler.

Harry turned to Beth, who was holding a beautiful conch shell she'd found and stuffed in her BC pocket. It was small but perfectly formed and without an inhabitant.

"Got you a present," she said, handing it to Harry.

Harry marveled at the shell for a minute, accepted it gratefully, and kissed her. "Thank you, baby," he said as he put it in his pocket. He wasn't sure if it was OK to remove it from the dive site, but he didn't want to risk any questions.

They arrived at the dock and made their way back to the condo. Little was said the entire way; both were completely exhausted. They didn't even shower. They just stripped off their bathing suits, collapsed in bed, and slept.

Chapter Thirteen

Harry and Beth decided to lounge around the pool and beach for the next few days. The sunsets were stunning, and the gentle breeze off the water kept the heat bearable. Cold drinks with tiny bamboo umbrellas seemed endless, and the bonfire kept the nights from getting too chilly. It crackled and popped, releasing tiny, glowing sparks that floated up like fireflies and disappeared into the night. The smell of coconut oil and the sound of steel-drum music in the distance were soothing reminders that they were on vacation.

This was the night. Harry had bought a ring and it was time to give it to Beth. He wanted to make it official. He was going to ask her there on the beach that night. He felt surprisingly nervous. His heart skipped a beat as he reached into the beach bag between the two lounge chairs they were relaxing in. He slowly fumbled through the towels and magazines until he reached the bottom and put his hand on the tiny box containing the symbol of the question that he wanted to ask her. His fingers wrapped around the tiny felt-covered cube and he mustered up his courage. Just as he started to pull it out, he heard a familiar voice.

"Harry, Beth—how you guys doin'?" André's voice broke the silence.

Harry dropped the box back to the bottom of the bag as he watched André walk over to them with a drink in his hand. Beth looked up at him, smiled, and invited him to join them. This totally blew the moment. Harry had his moves all worked out. He was going to roll out of the chair onto one knee and open the box. She would turn to him and smile with tears in her eyes and say, "Yes." But as André walked up, he thought, *This isn't the way I rehearsed this moment.* Of all the scenarios Harry had envisioned, this was not one of them.

André sat down across from them and settled in to talk to his most recent graduates. He spoke without the island accent, something that didn't slip past Beth.

"You sound different," she said, in a suspicious but friendly way.

"Yeah, I noticed it on the boat after the dive," Harry added.

André, in perfect English, confessed, "Yeah, I play it up for the tourists. It's good for business. People come here to escape reality for a while, and island charm adds to the fantasy. No harm, no foul."

Beth giggled, looking over her drink at André. "So what brings you down here?"

"I was walking down the beach to clear my head and saw the two of you sitting here so I thought I would say hello."

"Clearing your head?" Harry asked. "You live in an island paradise. You get to go diving in beautiful waters for a living. I'd think your head would be clear all the time."

"Yeah, one might think so, but times have been a little tough lately. People haven't been spending money the way they used to. It's hard for a little dive business to survive right now, but that's my problem, not yours." André then asked, "How are you enjoying your vacation? Have you been diving much?"

Beth took a deep breath and sighed. "Wonderful. We love it here. I wish I could stay here year 'round. We've been diving from the beach."

"Yeah," Harry added. "It seems like a lot more work than diving from the boat."

"You have time for another dive before you go home?" André asked.

Harry and Beth looked at each other. It was the perfect opportunity to get the pictures he wanted.

"Sure," he said, not waiting for an answer from Beth. Her excitement said it all for him.

"Tomorrow morning, we're heading to a nice wreck dive. It's close to shore, so we don't have to go too early. This is a three-hundred-thirty-foot Russian frigate that was sunk here for divers. It should be nice tomorrow, and it is an exciting dive. You interested?" André asked, looking directly at Harry.

"You bet. Maybe this time I'll remember my camera."

"Definitely," Beth added.

André gave them the information, said his goodbyes, and disappeared into the night.

The mood having been lost for the night, Harry decided to wait for another opportunity to pop the question. It was getting late, so they went back to the condo.

Entering the living room, Harry took Beth by the hand and led her to the shower. She loved being led like this, and she knew what was in store. He pulled her close and kissed her as they entered the shower together. The water poured over them as their hands explored each other. Harry maintained the kiss, his left hand pulling her by the small of her back tightly against him as his right hand tugged at the thin strings holding her bikini top in place. He turned around so the water was directly over her as he began to kiss her chin, then her neck, down her breasts, and slowly down her body as he removed her bikini bottoms.

Beth was enjoying every moment. She loved being manipulated by Harry in this gentle and passionate way. He knew exactly what to do and exactly when to do it. He'd seemed a bit preoccupied earlier, but she had his full attention now. She put her hands on his head and held on as Harry continued his journey down her firm, tanned body. The water pouring down kept her from being able to concentrate on Harry's movements, but Harry soon rewarded her patience with the direct attention that she now wanted so badly. She moaned aloud with pleasure as he continued the torture she so desired for what seemed like an eternity. Running her fingers through his hair, she soon felt her body tense up as waves of pleasure consumed her. She cried out, feeling herself completely lose control.

Harry, with the sense of accomplishment he always felt when he knew he'd pleased her, steadied her weak body in his strong arms. She was like a ragdoll, barely able to stand. His hands never left her as he began to bathe her with a soft sponge. He shampooed her hair and washed her limp body. She soon began to recover, her breathing back to normal. Then he showered himself, shut off the water, wrapped an oversized towel around her, and carried her to the bed, placing her on it without a word. Drying off, he joined her.

He wasn't looking for her to satisfy him; this time it was just about her. He wanted her to know she mattered, not for the pleasure she could give him, but for the joy she brought to his soul. He felt strong just being with her. Beth charged his batteries and filled his heart. There would be another opportunity to ask her to marry him, and he wanted it to be special. This was time to let this woman know that she was special.

He cuddled up behind her, holding her tightly, and they went to sleep. Tomorrow would be a busy day.

****

The next morning was chaotic. They awoke just in time to have breakfast, gather gear, get into swimsuits, and head to the boat. The new camera rested on top of Harry's gear bag by the front door of the condo. He didn't want to forget it this time.

They felt a little more like veteran divers this time. There would be no mistakes; he was sure of that. He blamed his previous mishap on the overwhelming feeling of the first dive. This was a new day and another dive.

Arriving at the boat, Harry handed the gear to André. After placing the bags on the deck, André put both hands out to help Beth make the crossing. He put his hands on her waist and spun her around as he took her from the dock, placing her firmly but gently on the deck. She laughed as she made the transition. It was the first time André had done anything that could have been construed as flirting with her. Then he reached out his hand to take Harry by the wrist and help him jump across.

Harry felt a little jealous as he watched Beth being swung around by André. Perhaps she enjoyed it a little too much. But when he reached his hand out for Harry, it all seemed harmless, and he thought he must have read too much into the gesture.

Taking a seat on the antiquated dive boat, Harry noticed that, besides the crew, there were only four other people onboard. There was a couple who looked scared to death, and the other two were what looked like college boys on a thrill-seeking trip. The boys were high fiving and psyching each other up.

"There's an accident waiting to happen," Harry muttered as he looked at Beth who was, by the way she looked at him, thinking the same thing.

Then, with a coy smirk, Harry nodded in their direction and said, "Sure you don't want to trade this forty-year-old in for two twenty-year-olds?"

"Not on your life. Been there, done that. Not interested," she replied.

The comment put Harry on top of the world. He smiled with a deep inner peace. He was happy, truly happy.

The other couple sat quietly, holding on as the boat tilted back and forth. They looked as though they were doing this on a dare and would rather be anywhere other than there.

The motor slowed to a dull drone as the captain approached the floating anchor buoy. The first mate tied off to the buoy, and the engine was silenced. The wind was dead calm, and it was amazing how quiet everything had become. It took some time for the gentle current to turn the boat around and put the slight tension on the line that held the boat in place.

André then began to take on his responsibility as dive master. "OK, guys. Has everyone met?" They took the question as a cue to introduce themselves.

The two boys were Joe and Tim. As suspected, they were on college break and wanted to hit the wreck while they were vacationing with their girlfriends, who wanted nothing to do with the dive, but would rather spend the time shopping with Daddy's credit cards. They didn't say, but they gave the impression they were trust fund kids looking to push the envelope.

The other couple, Anthony and Tanya, were on a needed vacation after finally getting the kids out of the house and off to college. They'd just retired and were looking for a little excitement. They seemed conservative and a little out of their element, but they were trying to expand their horizons.

André began to tell the group about the dive and review the safety rules. "Da ship now be in two sections; da bow be tilted up and apart from da main hull. Dere be access holes all through the ship for you to get out if you need to. Stay wit in sight of deese holes! I can't stress dat enough. And, stay wit in sight o your dive buddy. You be able to move through da ship, but be ready for da unexpected. It be possible you'll run into some of da ship's inhabitants. Dere be some big goliath grouper, moray eels, and maybe sharks. Don't mess wit dem. Give dem a wide berth and let dem go about dere business."

Harry and Beth turned to look at each other, smiling at the return of Andre's accent.

"We be going down all together and coming back all together. We will go down da anchor line to da bow of da boat, den we go our separate ways. Dere be a line from da stern of the boat what leads back to da surface at da anchor buoy. Dere be tanks of oxygen hanging on da safety stop lines at fifteen feet dat will help bleed off da nitrogen in da blood. Stay at dose tanks for five minutes, just for da safety. Total time limit for dis dive will be thirty minutes. Keep de eye on your dive computers. You know da rules; da deeper you go, da shorter da time. Dis be planned to be a no-deco dive. Let's keep it dat way. Dere be plenty to see at seventy feet. We jump in da water, we meet at da bow, I give you da sign to check your time. Twenty-eight minutes later, we be meeting at da stern and we be following da line back to da boat. Any questions?"

"How big are the goliath grouper on this wreck?" Anthony asked.

"Pretty big. Like da Harley Davidson, but wit fins and teeth," André replied.

"Awesome," the two boys said together.

"Don't mess wit dem. They be dangerous if provoked. You see dem getting mad and popping they tails, slowly back away," André insisted.

"Aaaa, you brought da camera dis time, Harry," André said. "You get a lots o nice shots down dere."

"Got it," Harry replied.

Then André turned to the group. "OK, time to be getting suited up and hit da water."

After a final equipment check, the divers hit the water and were on their way down the line. They formed a circle at the bow of the ship and André gave the signal to set their timers and watches for twenty-eight minutes. Then they were off on their own.

The two boys raced into the first open access they could find. Anthony and Tanya went down the port side, Harry and

Beth down the starboard. André hovered just above the ship. He'd led this dive many times before and liked it because he could keep track of the divers inside the wreck by the bubbles that escaped through hatches and access holes cut into the ship.

Harry felt much more comfortable on this dive. He was a bit reluctant to go into the ship, but when Beth went into a large window on the main deck, he followed.

Being in the ship underwater seemed unnatural. The inside of the ship was dark and covered with sea life, but obviously designed to be inhabited by people above the water. They'd entered the bridge. The ship's wheel was still in place, and Beth immediately went over and stood at the helm, giving Harry a perfect photo opportunity. The camera flashed and Beth came over to take the camera, signaling Harry to pose. He took a stance as if he were looking over the horizon as she snapped the shot. She hung on to the camera, and they headed to a hatch at the back of the large room.

Going through the inner hatch first, Harry took the lead with Beth close behind. The hatch opened into a corridor that ran lengthwise with the hull. The light coming in from the holes cut in the roof gave an eerie glow to the empty space, like streetlights in an alley, illuminating spots just below them with areas of darkness in between. Harry ventured down the corridor with Beth a short distance behind.

They found a room with an open hatch and went inside. It was the radio room. The dials and instruments on the walls, once alive with electricity, were now powerless. Speakers mounted to the bulkhead, formerly bustling with radio chatter, lay silent in the dark. They looked through the small room and, finding little of interest, Harry turned and headed back into the corridor.

He'd gone a few feet before he realized Beth hadn't come through the hatch. He decided to wait until she was right behind him.

That's when he saw it—a large, round, dark bulk in the corridor, just out of range of his clear vision. At first, Harry thought it was a large tank or barrel, but he could tell it was moving toward him. He could make out a line of spikes along the top and the white line from left to right as its mouth opened slightly. It was an enormous goliath grouper, and it looked much bigger than the Harley Davidson with fins and teeth that André had described. It looked like a car. It was as wide as the corridor and almost as tall.

Harry panicked and looked back for Beth, who was still in the radio room. When he turned back around, he found the fish had picked up speed and was headed right for him as though it were going to either attack or plow through him. It was so large that the only way to let it pass was to drop flat to the floor and let the monster pass overhead. Harry was breathing hard, using a lot of air, but the fish paused directly over Harry. He was trapped between the beast and the floor. Then, just as the claustrophobia was about to get the best of him, it began moving on rapidly.

Oh my god, Beth! raced through his mind as the fish took off. Harry turned back toward the radio room and looked for her. He was kicking frantically and again using up air fast. Breathing deeply, he found himself rising to the top of the corridor from the added buoyancy of his full lungs. His face was tense, which caused his mask to leak. Water was splashing around in the mask, getting in his eyes and nose, making him feel even more claustrophobic and adding to his panic.

Finally reaching the radio room, he found that Beth was not there. He headed back out the hatch and looked in horror at the camera Beth had been carrying lying on the floor. It was like a horrible omen.

He felt his heart sink into his stomach as he pictured his beautiful wife-to-be attacked by the Jurassic fish that had gotten between them. He wanted to scream out to her, but of course couldn't. He was helpless. He didn't know which way to turn or what to do. He was hyperventilating and finding it harder to breathe with each breath.

Then it became impossible to breathe at all. He looked at his pressure gauge and realized, to his horror that he'd used up all his air. *And this is how it ends,* he thought. He froze in the dark corridor, on the verge of tears as the carbon dioxide in his lungs became more than he could stand. He battled the growing urge to take a deep breath of sea water—a battle that he lost.

Just before he lost consciousness, he felt himself being jerked backward and up. He thought of the beast that had killed the love of his life and had now come back to finish him off as well.

Then, as he was jerked around, he felt a regulator being forced into his mouth and saw the welcome face of André shaking him back to reality. He choked, coughed, and vomited into the regulator, struggling to regain his breathing.

André put his secondary regulator into his own mouth and tried to calm Harry down. Harry cleared his mask the way he was taught, and the two started toward one of the escape holes cut into the top of the corridor.

Harry felt himself on the edge of tears as he emerged from the ship with André. He then saw the two other couples were there, waiting to assist if needed, along with another diver in pink dive gear. It was Beth. She was OK.

André controlled the ascent by holding on to the shoulder straps of Harry's BC, releasing bursts of the expanding air trying to pull Harry to the surface. Harry just relaxed and focused on his breathing. He felt embarrassed about having to be rescued, but was glad André was there. He owed him his life, and he knew it.

They reached the fifteen-foot stop lines. André took the regulator for the oxygen tank and motioned for Harry to replace his regulator with it. Harry pulled the concentrated oxygen deeply into his lungs. They remained there until the tank was running low, just as a precaution. Better safe than sorry. Once out of the water, nothing could prevent the bends, but the oxygen helped leach the concentrated nitrogen out of his blood.

Back on the boat, Harry felt lucky to be alive. He was still breathing oxygen from an emergency tank kept on the boat. The other divers were looking on, trying in vain not to add to his embarrassment, and Beth was right beside him.

"I thought it got you," Harry said.

"No way. I popped into the corridor and saw it right in front of me, so I went through the escape hole above. It didn't move, so I couldn't get back down to you. André saw me and came to help," Beth answered.

"I saw the camera on the deck and thought the worst," Harry added.

"This camera?" she said, holding it up for him to see.

"You went back and got it," he said with surprise.

"Yep," she said, preparing to take another picture of him.

"I thought I'd lost you."

"No chance," she said, lowering the camera and putting her arm around him "You're stuck with me."

"I love you," Harry said, on the verge of tears again.

André, seeing the sappy scene, walked up, took the oxygen mask off Harry's face, and said, "OK, OK, that's about enough oxygen for you."

Setting the oxygen aside, and with the accent long forgotten he asked, "You OK, bud?"

"Yeah, I'm OK. Looks like you could make a career out of saving my ass," Harry replied.

"No doubt," André said. "I want you to get checked out when we get back, just in case. I had to bring you up pretty quick."

"I will."

"I'm serious, Harry. Just leave your gear with me. I'll take care of it. You can pick it up from the dive shop tomorrow. OK?"

"OK."

The captain fired up the engine, and they were on their way. The sun was blazing, and the wind had picked up, so the ride back was a bit rough. Harry was glad when they got their feet back on dry land.

"See you, André," Harry said, turning to leave.

"Take care, Harry. Don't forget to get checked out."

"He will, André. I promise," Beth said.

They were on their way home when Beth told the cab driver to take them to the hospital.

Harry looked at Beth and said, "I'm fine."

"Now, you just heard me promise, didn't you?" she said in a commanding tone.

"Yeah," he responded.

The cab pulled up to the small hospital. Harry paid the driver, and they got out.

Harry felt that he was wasting everyone's time, but Beth insisted they continue. They went inside and found things different than hospitals they'd been to in the past. It was smaller, and the atmosphere was more relaxed. The doctors and nurses were going about their business calmly with smiles on their faces. The waiting room was painted a cool, tropical green and, best of all, it was empty.

Arriving at the check-in desk, Harry was surprised to find the triage nurse was expecting him.

"You must be Harry," she said.

"André called?" Beth asked.

"Yes, he did," she replied, handing Harry a clipboard. "He wants to make sure you're OK. I need you to fill this out for me."

"I feel I'm wasting everyone's time," Harry said, taking the clipboard.

"No, you're not wasting anyone's time. André said you'd had to ascend too quickly. You could have effects long after the event. We would rather treat you for that now than for a stroke or worse later," the nurse said.

Harry suddenly didn't feel so foolish. He filled out the paperwork and returned the clipboard to the nurse, then was taken back for the usual tests. A young doctor entered the room and introduced himself.

"Hello, Harry. I'm Doctor Spellman," he said, shaking hands.

"Hello, doc," Harry replied.

"How you feelin'?"

"Except for a headache, I feel fine."

"Headache?" the doctor asked with interest. "Describe the pain."

"It's a steady pressure."

"When did it start?"

"On the boat. On the way back," Harry said. "Is that bad?"

"Probably not, but I would rather be safe than sorry. We're going to do a CT scan to be sure."

"You're the doctor," Harry said.

"Do you want me to share information with your wife?"

Harry paused for a moment at the word "wife." She wasn't his wife. Not yet. But he could see how others thought she was. They were so attuned to each other now that they might as well be married. Did he want the doctor to give her information?

"I think if there was a problem, I would rather tell her. I'm fine anyway."

"OK, let's get started."

For the next couple of hours, Harry was poked and prodded and shoved into a huge buzzing doughnut that would slice him into small slivers—without a scratch. When it was all through, he was escorted to the doctor's office and asked to wait.

****

Dr. Spellman sat in the X-Ray room and viewed the images as they appeared on the monitor. He sipped his coffee and watched as, one by one, the slices of Harry's brain came into view. As the images progressed, a small dot appeared. On the next slice, it was larger. The next revealed what looked like a tentacle protruding from the dot. The next one was worse. "Damn," he muttered.

****

Doctor Spellman walked into the office where Harry sat.

"Well, doc, what's the verdict?" Harry asked, confidently.

"How's your headache, Harry?"

"It's fading, but still there," Harry responded. Suddenly, he felt a bit of alarm. He was thinking back to the dive classes and the dangers of a rapid ascent.

Dr. Spellman, sensing Harry's tension, said "Well, Harry, there was no damage from the dive."

Harry was relieved, but that relief was short-lived.

"From the dive? It sounds like there's something else."

The doctor sat down at his desk and asked, "How have you been feeling lately?"

"Fine, doc," Harry said, his uneasiness increasing. "What's going on?"

"Feeling run down? Lethargic at all?"

"A little bit. But I am getting older. Tell me, doc. What's going on?"

This was the part of his profession he hated. "We found something on the CT scan we need to talk about." Dr. Spellman walked around the desk with a file of images. He spread them out on a light box in sequence and pointed to a mass that was woven through the brain tissue. It looked somewhat like an octopus. He explained, "It's a tumor, Harry, and it's bad."

Harry looked at the images with disbelief. There it was. There was no doubt. It looked so odd. He didn't understand how this could be. How could this be in his head without him knowing about it?

"Oh, my god," Harry gasped. His thoughts shifted to cancer patients he'd seen in the past. The suffering, the sickness, the weakness. He didn't want to go out like that. He wanted to ask if there had been a mistake, but the evidence was clear.

"Did you tell Beth?" he asked.

"No, Harry. I wanted to talk to you alone."

"What, what do we do about it?" Harry asked, trying to keep his composure.

"First thing, Harry, you need to see your doctor back home. You and he will have to put together a treatment plan."

"I guess I should cut my vacation short," he muttered.

"Harry, finish your vacation," Dr. Spellman responded. "You feel pretty good, right?"

"Yeah, I feel fine, but shouldn't I get back home and get started on treatment?"

"Harry, a couple of weeks won't make any difference. Enjoy your vacation and see your doctor when you get home."

"What are my chances?"

"I'm not an oncologist, Harry. Anything I would say would be a guess."

"Guess," Harry persisted.

"I don't want to guess. Wait until you see an oncologist," Dr. Spellman insisted.

"I'm done for, aren't I?"

"OK, Harry, since you insist. It doesn't look good. The tumor is deep in the brain and spread throughout the tissue in such a way that it appears to be inoperable. You can try to fight it with chemo and radiation, and there are new treatments discovered all the time. You shouldn't give up hope, but it is bad. Make the best use of the time you have."

Harry sat, startled with the frankness of the news, then gathered his composure and stood up.

"Thank you. I appreciate your candor."

"Good luck, Harry, and don't give up."

"I won't," Harry said as he turned and walked toward the office door.

He met Beth, who put her arm around him. After a bit of paperwork at the front desk, they were on their way.

"So I guess you didn't get injured," she said.

He'd been worried about telling her what the doctor had found and was relieved that she'd given him an out. "No injury."

"Fantastic. I knew you were OK," she responded. "Now aren't you glad you got checked out? Now we know."

"Yep, now I know," Harry amended.

They walked out of the hospital and took a cab back to the condo. Harry was quiet, trying to figure how he could keep up appearances with Beth until he was ready to tell her…if he would ever be ready to tell her. He was going to die. How do you tell the woman you love—the woman you were going to ask to marry you—that you're going to die, and soon? How do you break her heart like that?

But I'm not dead yet! he thought. *I have money, I have power, and I have resources. I'm not one of the masses without options. I will find a way. This was one doctor's opinion. There are other doctors, better doctors, and I can afford them.* He smiled to himself as he pushed all this to the back of his mind and relaxed with Beth in the back of the cab.

"Ready to leave the islands?" Harry asked.

"Time to go home already?" she asked, with a hint of disappointment. Her exaggerated, pouty lip always got his blood boiling with excitement.

"Who said anything about going home?" he responded. "We still have two months left."

"Where are we going next?"

"You'll see" he said with confidence.

Chapter Fourteen

Harry and Beth arrived in Kenya late in the evening. They found their guide, Reggie, waiting for them as they got off the plane. The usual introductions were made and Reggie led them to a dusty, though very nice, Land Rover.

Reggie was a safari guide and dressed the part. A stocky, older man, slightly grey at the temples, he had leathery skin with wrinkles that formed a road map across his face. One could tell he'd spent most of his life in the harsh African sun. His khaki shirt and shorts were badly wrinkled and looked as though he'd slept in them, but they were clean and only bore the traces of the day's work behind him. His fedora was typical for a hunting guide, with a snakeskin band around the crown. He was covered in light dust and looked tired, but he did his best to smile as he welcomed them.

Reggie placed their bags in the back of the Land Rover and closed the hatch. They climbed in and headed to the clubhouse that would be their home. After the flight, it was nice to settle into the comfort of the vehicle. The sounds and smells of airports and long hours on planes had taken their toll. They were ready to sleep.

Harry leaned back in the corner and placed his arm around Beth as she leaned into him. He held her securely as the smooth road became rugged terrain. They were headed through the wilderness toward the darkness of the African night. The absence of lights accentuated the starlit sky.

"Your first time in Africa?" Reggie asked.

"Yes, it is," Beth responded.

"You're gonna love it here," Reggie said as he pulled out of the parking lot. "We have a room ready for you."

Harry looked at the stars and began to dwell on what he'd learned in the hospital. He thought about the life he'd just begun and how he was told that it was likely to end soon. He thought about all the work he'd done in his life and how inconsequential it all was. Gazing at the stars, he wondered if there was a God as he was raised to believe, and if so, why he was doing this to him. And he thought about the beautiful young woman in his arms who had made his life really worth living. He wanted to marry her. But if he did, she would have to watch him die. Was that fair to her?

He decided to wait to propose until he knew more. He thought she knew he was going to ask her. He could see it in her eyes every time they spoke, and he almost did ask her that evening on the beach, but fate had intervened. He would wait until he saw some specialists and come up with a treatment plan. Once he knew everything would be OK, he would then enter a new chapter in his life—the life with Beth that he really wanted. He would make her his wife.

Arriving at the resort, the couple marveled at the contrast of its well-manicured grounds with the wild country surrounding it. It was like Shangri-La, hidden from the rest of the world, a large three-story, cabin-style building with a solid, rugged, but high quality design, decorated in a hunting theme, which made the guests feel they were getting their money's worth. The main house was centered on the property with a circular driveway in front of it. It was about one hundred feet wide, and the outside lights gave it a majestic glow in the thick darkness. On one side was a large barn, on the other, an oversized garage.

The Land Rover came to a halt in front of the main house. Reggie said, "Here we are," and climbed out. He immediately opened the rear passenger door, took Beth's hand, and helped her out.

Beth, who'd been dozing, was suddenly confronted with the magnificence of the resort. Her eyes took it all in. "Wow!" was all she was able to manage.

Harry, climbed out of the Land Rover, paused and looked around. "Nice place, Reggie."

"We call it home," Reggie replied. He turned to Motaba, one of the staff, and motioned him to get the bags out of the back. Then he led them through the oversized double doors that opened into the huge entryway. He turned and muttered something quietly to Motaba, turned to the couple and said, "You go ahead and get settled in. Motaba will show you your room. When you wake up, come down for breakfast, and we'll talk about your safari."

"OK, Reggie. See you in the morning," Harry said.

"Night," was all Beth could manage.

Inside the common area, the ceiling went up to the three-story roof. The interior was of hand-hewn wood, carefully fit, and finished with no detail overlooked. The furnishings were rustic—oversized chairs and heavy wooden tables. Heads of the game animals killed over the years hung on the walls. Centered in the back wall was a massive stone fireplace with an enormous mantle. Curved staircases rose up both sides of the room, leading to the guest rooms that were on the upper floors.

They followed their bags up to the top floor and into a suite. The room was oversized and very comfortable with a large living room and a complete kitchen area. It had luxurious leather furniture, the arrangement of which focused attention on a stone fireplace. The décor was African art—shields, spears, and ceremonial masks—placed around the quarters. Another door led to the bedroom.

As they entered the bedroom, they paused to take it in. It was absolutely beautiful. All the furnishings were oversized and extremely ornate, made of hand-carved wood and stone. The mirror over the dresser was at least six feet tall and five feet wide, bordered with a carved frame. In the center of the room was a raised platform about a foot high and at least five feet larger on all sides than the massive canopy bed it supported. The bed itself was like the rest of the furniture in the room—oversized and over the top. It was nine feet tall and had fine, white mosquito netting drawn up to each corner like a curtain. The bed was covered in satin sheets and a satin comforter with a tiger-stripe pattern that complemented the room's décor.

Beth looked up at Harry just as he looked down at her, both of them in awe, and smiled.

Motaba walked in, placed the bags on the floor next to the dresser, and turned to them. He, having seen this room many times, was unaffected by its quality. He showed them the room's features and then turned to leave. Harry reached into his pocket to tip him, but Motaba declined.

"Thank you, sir, but that isn't necessary. Please enjoy your stay, and if there is anything that you need, please ask. My name is Motaba."

Motaba left the room, and they were finally alone. They looked around a little more but, exhausted, turned to the bed. Agreeing that they wanted to sleep in, they disrobed and cuddled up on the soft, comfortable mattress. They wanted to make love, but the day's events had worn them out. It wasn't long until they were asleep.

Harry usually dreamed of work or business, but lately his dreams had changed. He dreamed of adventure and excitement. Money and power took a back seat to Beth and the island, of floating weightless through the water, and of the giant fish he thought had taken his love. But tonight, he dreamed of Africa, of drums beating and tribal ceremonies, of tigers and lions, of elephants and wildebeests, of the African sunsets he'd yet to see.

After what seemed like moments, it was morning and he was awake, fully refreshed, and raring to go.

Beth was still asleep as Harry slipped out of bed and went over to the kitchen area and put on a pot of coffee. He showered in a unique stone enclosure. Emerging from the bathroom, he found Beth awake, lying on the bed with her coffee in hand. Harry was drying his hair with a towel, walking toward her with another towel around his waist. She motioned to a cup on the table next to the bed that she'd fixed the way he liked it. He bent down to kiss her and picked up the cup.

"My turn," she said, as she slipped out of the bed and made her way to the bathroom.

"You're going to love the shower," he said, watching her smooth, sexy body disappear from sight. He loved her walking around naked in the morning. She was so comfortable in her body, so confident, so uninhibited. She was a joy to be around.

Harry turned his attention to the luggage and began to unpack. He put clothes in the dresser and in the closet. He was almost finished when he felt soft hands sliding around his waist from behind and moving up his chest to squeeze him tightly.

"Motaba," he said coyly. "Beth is in the shower. I told you to meet me later."

"Oooh, so now I have to compete with the help, huh? I hope you two are very happy together," Beth replied, pulling away.

Harry turned and grabbed her, pulling her close with one hand around her waist and the other on the back of her neck. She was wrapped in one towel with another spun into a makeshift turban around her still-wet hair. He kissed her passionately as he pulled the towel from her hair. The wet hair, her beautiful green eyes, and the wanton expression on her face made her look like an animal, a predator, and Harry was her prey.

She grabbed the towel around his waist and dragged him toward the oversized bed. She turned him around, pushed him as hard as she could onto the bed, and climbed on at his feet.

She grabbed the knot in Harry's towel and ripped it open. Harry was instantly aroused. She crawled over him like a lioness on the prowl, ripping off the towel covering her, and let her hair fall down onto his chest. She stared into his eyes as she took him inside her.

Later, as they lay together, Harry's thoughts drifted. There were many other places he wanted to go and many things he wanted to do on this vacation, but the tumor in his head needed attention. He thought about how things had changed. He felt a bit more fatigued, but it had come on so slowly that he hadn't even noticed it. Was that a symptom? And there were the headaches—the doctor made note of that. He didn't know what he was dealing with. He decided to put it out of his mind for the remainder of the trip and go at it full-force when he got back. He had money, and money gives you options.

Harry kissed the back of her neck. "You ready to start the day, baby?"

"I thought we just did," she replied.

"I was talking about breakfast."

"I'm starving."

"Me too," Harry said as he climbed out of bed and stretched.

Beth slowly rose from the bed, starring at Harry the entire time. She liked watching him walk through the room naked, too. And she knew that when she moved around naked, his eyes were glued to her. The voyeuristic behavior made her feel sexy. Both watching and being watched. She passed him on the way back to the bathroom and slapped his naked ass as he stretched.

"Ouch," he said with surprise. He tried to retaliate, but Beth was too fast for him.

She shut the bathroom door, giggling, and began to dry her hair. "I won't be long."

****

The main room of the lodge was equally breathtaking in the morning. As they made their way down the stairs, they were met by Reggie, who was dressed the same way he was the previous night, but without the dust, dirt, and wrinkles. His khakis were pressed and clean, and he was obviously rested and refreshed, too.

"Morning, folks!" he offered. "I trust you slept well."

"Like a baby," Beth said.

"Great," Reggie said, turning toward the dining room. "Let's get some breakfast."

The three of them went into the large dining room. The table and chairs were like those in the rest of the house. They sat down and a woman appeared, pouring coffee for them and asking what they'd like for breakfast.

Reggie asked, "What would you like? You name it, and it will be prepared for you."

They ordered, and Reggie began to go over the plans for the day. "Are you both planning to hunt?"

The question reminded Harry of the reason that they were there. He looked at Beth, waiting for her response. She declined, never having considered killing an animal. "No, this is Harry's adventure. I'm just here to watch." She wasn't sure she could even watch, but was excited to be a part of what was going on.

"Just me, then," Harry said.

"OK. What kind of game are you after?"

Harry paused at the question. It hadn't occurred to him that there would be a choice to make. He looked at Beth and Reggie, both of whom were waiting for his answer. Then it came to him. It didn't matter what kind of game. He thought of the pictures in Stan's office. He could remember seeing Stan standing over an animal he killed, but couldn't remember what kind of animal it was. Did it matter? Was he here to take home a stuffed head? The answer was obvious.

"Adventure!" Harry replied. "I don't care what type of game we come across. I'm here to enjoy the safari, no matter the game."

Reggie smiled. "OK. After breakfast we'll ride over to the shooting range."

Feeling that he finally had a handle on the day, Harry relaxed and sipped his coffee. Breakfast soon arrived.

"Are we the only ones here, Reggie?" Harry asked.

"No, Harry. There are two other hunters here. They're out on the plains now. We have to start before dawn to get a good hunt. They were out of here just a few hours after you arrived."

Turning to Beth, Reggie added, "You are the only lady here. Wives don't often come along."

"Do they usually hunt?" she asked.

"Sometimes. Mostly they want to make sure of the type of game their husbands are after, if you know what I mean."

It took a second for Beth to get the joke. Then she smiled.

"So, this is your first safari, correct?"

"Yes, it is," Harry responded.

"What caught your interest?"

Harry, not wanting to go into too much detail, said "Well, Reggie, I've worked hard all my life, and I figured it was time to live a little."

"Here, here!" Reggie replied, holding up his coffee cup in a toast.

****

Later, on the shooting range, Reggie opened the back of the Land Rover, revealing an assortment of rifles and pistols he'd brought for Harry to shoot.

"I want you to get a feel for these weapons, Harry. The game you decide to harvest will determine the weapon," Reggie said, handing him a rifle.

"Harvest?" Beth interrupted.

"That's what we call it when you kill an animal," he replied.

Harry then took the rifle and instinctively put it to his shoulder. Looking through the scope, he saw the crosshairs pinpointing the spot where the round would strike. He'd never held a big rifle before. It gave him a feeling of power. Looking downrange through the scope, he could see a large target. Excitement flooded his body. He was really going to do this.

"Have you ever shot a weapon before, Harry?" Reggie asked.

"I've shot a small pistol a couple of times, but I've never fired a rifle."

"OK. This is a bit different. A pistol is for short range. A rifle is designed for distance. They have more power and recoil, but you have more control. Understand?"

"Got it."

"First things first. Safety!" Reggie began to teach the couple about the finer workings of the Remington 700 that Harry was holding: how to load and unload it, how to check the barrel for obstructions, how to hold it properly and, most importantly, good safety practices. Then it was time to make some noise. Reggie handed each of them earmuffs and safety glasses, and they walked up to a makeshift table at the shooting line.

"Now this is a two-seventy caliber," Reggie said, pulling a box of rounds from his pocket. "It has a kick, so remember to hold it tightly against your shoulder. I'll shoot it first so you can see what to expect, OK?"

"OK," they replied together.

"Line is going hot!" Reggie yelled. Then he opened the bolt, placed a round in the breach, and slid the bolt forward, forcing the round into the chamber. He slid the thumb safety back into "safe" position. He turned his head to the couple and said, "Eyes and ears, boys and girls."

Harry and Beth slid their earmuffs and safety glasses into place and prepared for the blast. The rifle looked small, almost like a toy, not at all what Harry expected. But when Reggie shouldered the rifle, slid off the safety, and gently squeezed the trigger, the report from the rifle showed it was no toy.

The target slid down behind a berm that Harry didn't see. It was as if it had disappeared into the ground.

"Where did it go?" Beth asked.

"It's getting spotted," Reggie said. "Watch."

Just then, the target slid back up with a large white spot dead-center of the bulls-eye. A moment later, the target went down again. The spot was removed, the hole was taped, and the target returned.

"Who is doing that?" Beth asked.

"Motaba. It's called pulling butts. Don't worry. He's safe down there."

He handed the rifle to Harry with the bolt open. Harry took the rifle and stood where Reggie had stood. He yelled, "Line is going hot!" as Reggie did, pushed a round into the breach, slid it home with the bolt, and slid on the safety. He raised the rifle to his shoulder and looked through the scope. Finding the target, he placed the crosshairs on it and slid off the safety. He was starting to squeeze the trigger when his body tensed up. He was anticipating the shot and when it went off, it startled him. The recoil wasn't quite as bad as he'd thought. The target slid out of site and reappeared a moment later with a black spot on the lower left-hand corner.

Beth giggled a little, but didn't want to hurt Harry's feelings.

"Not bad, Harry," Reggie said. "Most people don't even hit the target with their first shot."

Harry felt his pride return with the comment. He looked at Beth and smiled. The target went down and came back up with the spot gone and the hole taped. Harry put another round in, preparing to take another shot.

"Remember to keep it tight against your shoulder. Take a deep breath, let half of it out, then squeeze off the shot," Reggie said, coaching Harry.

Harry put the rifle to his shoulder and followed Reggie's advice. He squeezed off the round and waited as the target slid out of sight. It took only seconds for the target to return, but it seemed like hours, during which they could have heard a pin drop. And there it was—a big white spot on the target just inches from the center. Beth jumped up and down, clapping her hands. Harry's chest expanded with pride. Reggie was impressed.

"Well done, young man. Let's do that again," Reggie said.

After a few more shots, Reggie took the rifle, cleared it, and said, "Let's try something a little bigger." He pulled another rifle out of its case. It looked very similar to the Remington 700, except it didn't have a front or rear site on the barrel, which was larger in diameter.

"This is a seven-millimeter Remington Magnum. It works the same, but has a bit more wallop than the two-seventy." He opened the breach to clear the weapon and handed it to Harry.

Harry looked at the weapon and wasn't too worried—until he saw the cartridge. It was twice the size.

Reggie, seeing that Harry was done looking at it, took it back. "OK, Harry, I'll shoot it first, and then you can give it a go." He put the round in the breach, slid the bolt home, and yelled to prepare Motaba for more firing. He raised the rifle to his shoulder, pulled it in tight, took a deep breath, let out half of it, and pulled the trigger. The silence was broken by a thundering explosion. There was a bright flash at the end of the muzzle, and the rifle jerked backwards, as did Reggie's shoulder. The target slid down in the butts and, after a few seconds, returned with a hit just to the right of the center. Reggie pulled the bolt back, ejected the empty shell from the chamber, and handed the rifle to Harry.

Not wanting to be outdone, Harry accepted it and stepped up to the line. He put a round in the chamber, shouldered the rifle, and took the shot. The target disappeared and returned with a spot close to center. Harry, having had enough abuse to his shoulder for one day, handed the rifle back.

"Well done," Reggie said.

He put the rifle back in the Land Rover and yelled to Motaba, "Line's going cold."

Then they went to a shorter range. There were steel targets on spinners about fifty feet away. Reggie opened a box he'd brought from the Land Rover and placed it on a table strategically located at the firing line. He took an array of handguns out, placed them on the table, opened an ammo box, and set out ammunition for the various weapons and then turned his attention to Harry.

"You said you'd fired a pistol before. Do you know what caliber?" Reggie asked.

"I think it was a twenty-two," Harry replied.

"Ok, this will be different," Reggie said as he handed Harry a forty-five caliber automatic. "It has a bit more kick and is a lot louder."

They spent the next few hours shooting a variety of handguns—the .45 automatic, to several .44 magnums, and a .454 Casull.

Beth wasn't planning to hunt but would have to carry a sidearm for protection in the bush. So it would be necessary for her to get used to it. Beth and Harry decided they liked the forty-five automatic best.

Reggie took the firearms, put them back in their cases, and put away the remaining ammunition. Turning back to Harry and Beth, he said, "Let's head for the barn." The trio made it back around one p.m. and went to the dining room for lunch.

"So, Harry, what did you think of your first shooting lesson?" Reggie asked as they ate.

"Very impressive," Harry replied, rubbing his shoulder. "One shot of that seven millimeter was enough."

"If you place it properly, it is enough."

"So what's on the agenda for the rest of the day, Reggie?" Beth asked.

"The rest of the day is yours, folks. Feel free to roam the grounds, swim in the pool, or just lounge in the main room, but don't miss the sunset. It's spectacular."

They finished their lunch and decided to go up to their suite and take a much-needed nap. The sun, the heat, and the shooting had taken tolls on them, and they were still experiencing a bit of jet lag. The time zone was so far off what they were used to that it felt like midnight to them. It would probably take a day or so, but their bodies would get used to it.

They awoke that evening and made their way out to the back deck of their suite. The sun was already down, and only a slight glow remained on the horizon. The stillness of the night was broken by the sound of insects calling to each other. The deck was screened to prevent their intrusion into the guests' sanctuary, but the sound was still intense.

Looking down, they could see a Land Rover and a four-by-four truck parked next to a primitive-looking concrete structure. The tailgate of the truck was open, and there was what looked like blood in its bed. The yellow fluorescent lights designed to keep the mosquitoes away made the blood look pitch black. A small group of people were gathered at the scene, and activity was going on inside the structure.

The two made their way downstairs and out back to see what was going on. When they arrived, what they saw brought home the reality of the hunt. A large kudu—a type of antelope—was hanging from a hand-powered gambrel winch by its rear legs as one of the staff was skinning it. Off to the side was a table holding tools covered in blood. The animal had been field dressed, and the scene was a bit much for Beth. She held on to Harry's arm as they approached.

The hunter who had bagged the animal was off to one side, looking on like a supervisor at a construction site. From his demeanor, it was apparent it was not his first kill. He was unaffected by the blood and gore, as were the staff. But as someone who'd spent most of his life in an office, Harry was a little shocked.

Reggie was talking to the man with a drink in his hand, but excused himself when he noticed Harry and Beth. He walked over and greeted them as if nothing was going on.

"What do you think, Harry? Nice kill, huh?" Reggie exclaimed.

"Yeah," Harry replied. He was trying not to seem overwhelmed but was doing a poor job of it.

Reggie, seeing how it was affecting the couple, led them back to the main house. "I know it's a bit overwhelming when you see it the first time, but you're coming in at the wrong time. The thrill of the hunt, the tracking, taking the shot, and loading it into the truck, all go a long way toward preparing you for the end."

"What kind of animal was that?" Harry asked.

"It's a kudu," Reggie responded. "A very difficult kill. They have keen senses and are easily spooked. That one was a good forty-eight incher."

"A forty-eight incher?" Beth asked.

"That's the length of the antlers—the bigger, the better. That one had antlers measuring just over forty-eight inches long and very wide at the base," Reggie explained.

Harry was glad to hear her say something. She no longer looked shocked. She was shaken, but stronger than he'd given her credit for. But was he strong enough to handle it himself? He had to admit the gory scene shocked him a little, but it also excited him. The thing that worried him was the initial effect it had on Beth. He loved the way she looked at him and wondered if killing an animal would change that look.

They went back to the house, sat down in front of the fireplace, and ordered a drink. A slow fire crackled, burning off the slight chill of the evening. They were comfortable and discussed their plans for the next day.

They decided to get outfitted with the proper attire for the hunt in the morning, and then to go on a scouting drive through the countryside to ease them into the rigors of the hunt. They would be spending days in the bush, and it's difficult for newcomers to the Dark Continent. Sleeping in tents was a far cry from the luxury of the lodge. They listened to Reggie's stories about other hunters and the close calls they'd had: stories of lions taking game in the camp when all were asleep, of hunters coming so close to a bull elephant they almost became a statistic. But all the stories had happy endings, everyone going home safe and sound.

Harry thought of life in the city and how things he thought of as dangers there hardly compared to the perils of life in the bush. When people in the city ran into trouble, they could be sued, have their car towed, or lose their job. People in the bush could become lion food or an elephant footprint, or get lost and die from exposure or dehydration. This land was the real deal. He wished he could tell a story that would impress Reggie the way Reggie's stories impressed him, but nothing that he'd ever done could compare with an average day in the African wilderness.

It was getting late and Beth, who'd been mesmerized by the fireside conversation, yawned, indicating she was ready for bed. Harry was tired too, so they said their goodnights and went to their suite.

Beth went straight into the shower and Harry turned down the bed. Grabbing a couple of towels, he joined Beth in the shower. As Beth exited, Harry stayed in to let the hot water massage his shoulder, sore from the recoil of rifles.

After Beth left the bathroom, she went to the dresser to brush out her hair. Harry had emptied the travel bag containing her cosmetics, hairbrushes, and such, placing them in the dresser drawers. The first drawer she came to held Harry's stuff. She was about to close the drawer when she saw something that looked out of place. It was a little felt-covered box with a domed top. She stared at it with excitement. There was no doubt what it was.

She looked toward the shower and, seeing Harry was still enjoying the hot water, she turned back to the box. He was obviously going to pop the question. She stared at the box for a moment, unsure what to do. She wanted to see it; the curiosity was killing her. She reached in to grab it, but just before touching it drew her hand back.

She wanted to be surprised when Harry finally gave it to her. But her curiosity was strong, and she reached in again and touched the box. As she started to take it out of the drawer she heard the shower turn off, so she dropped it and closed the drawer. She decided it was for the best. After all, she now knew he'd bought the ring; it would just be a matter of time until he asked her. She hoped that the excitement of seeing the ring for the first time would be enough to convince Harry she hadn't spoiled the surprise.

She opened another drawer, found the hairbrushes, and hurriedly began to brush out her hair. Sitting in front of the mirror, she reflected on the course of events that had brought her here. She looked at herself, how she had grown up. She remembered sitting in her bedroom in front of her dresser, brushing her hair, dreaming of being grown up, wondering who would be her Prince Charming, wondering what it would be like to be swept off her feet, wondering how her true love would propose and change their lives forever.

Now those questions would soon be answered; she would soon live that dream. She knew who. Now she just had to wait for when and the how. She brushed her hair vigorously, smiling to herself with her newfound knowledge. This was a secret…it was Harry's secret…and she decided to keep the fact that she now knew about it…a secret!

Harry emerged from the bathroom with a towel wrapped around his waist. She watched him in the mirror, seeing him differently now, as her husband, not just her boyfriend. She almost wished she'd not seen the box and was glad she didn't get a chance to open it. As it was, she felt that in some way she'd betrayed him. This was something that he had planned, and she'd cheapened it. Not on purpose, of course, but cheapened it just the same. She'd have to keep her cool and forget about it until he made his move. She hoped it would be soon.

She joined Harry in bed. Sliding in behind him, she wrapped one arm around his chest and one leg over his waist.

He loved when she did that, and they went to sleep, a sleep that, for Harry, was filled with the tales of adventure told to him by Reggie: a sleep filled with dreams of lions and elephants, of baboons and zebras.

But Beth dreamed of a black-felt box, and of it being opened for her by the man she loved. It was a long, long night.

Chapter Fifteen

The darkness of the night gave way to streams of orange and gold as the sun rose above the African horizon. Rays of light pierced thin stratus clouds, stretching from the heavens as if forced through a giant stencil.

Reggie met Harry and Beth and led them to what Reggie called "the whiskey locker," the back half of the barn located to one side of the main house, which held all the gear used in the field. Shelves from floor to ceiling were loaded with equipment. The whiskey locker contained everything from canteens to tents, from pocket compasses to off-road trailers. Anything that a person would need to survive in the wild was accounted for, organized, and neatly shelved. There were also racks of new and used khaki clothing and boots of all sizes. Reggie motioned to the clothing and had Harry and Beth pick out what they thought would fit. Then he went about running down his checklist, as he'd done hundreds of times before. He loaded equipment into the Land Rover and began to fill up a trailer. They were going to make their home in a tent for the next few days, and it was a long way back to get something forgotten.

The first thing Harry grabbed was a fedora, putting it on his head. Beth looked at it and giggled. She found shorts and blouses in her size and tried them on in a small dressing room. She was amazed at everything here; it was like a department store. They found enough clothes for the trip and put them in the car. Reggie gave each of them a hunting knife and a compass, two canteens, a cartridge belt, a mess kit, binoculars, a flint and steel, and a small backpack.

The trailer was loaded and hitched to the Land Rover and pulled around to the front of the lodge. The trio went into the dining room for a big breakfast.

"So what's our plan?" Harry asked Reggie.

"Well, Harry, we're going to go scout around for a couple of days to find where the animals are and where they're going. I don't expect we'll be taking game this trip, just scouting to see what you'd like to harvest. But if the opportunity presents itself, the hunt is on. We'll be back in a few days, but there's nothing around for miles, so if you need it, bring it!"

After breakfast, the three of them met up with Motaba, piled into the Land Rover and headed out on their pre-adventure adventure. They drove for hours and finally settled on the rim of a valley. It was dry and hot, and to Harry, it didn't look any different than the trails that they had been on since they left the lodge.

"This it?" Harry asked.

"This is it," Reggie replied as he and Motaba looked through binoculars, scanning for signs of game.

From the rim of the valley you could see for miles. A small oasis was in the middle of it where water from the rainy season was trapped, providing migrating animals with precious drinking water. There were patches of high grass and trees, and a group of dots around the watering hole were actually a herd of wildebeest.

Reggie and Motaba were in their own world for a few moments as they scanned the valley, looking for game and predators. This was their specialty and they knew the job. The last thing they wanted to do was to set up camp too far away from their objective or too close to a pride of hungry lions. They muttered for a few moments, pointing to objects in the distance. After they'd agreed on what they'd discussed, Motaba unpacked the gear and Reggie came back to Beth and Harry.

"Everything all right, Reggie?" Harry asked.

"Right as rain, Harry," he replied. "Let's get the camp set up."

They cleared the area and began to set up the tents which, with the Land Rover and trailer, formed a wide circle. All the tent openings faced the center. Once that was completed, the next task was to find firewood.

Reggie handed Harry a holster with a .45 caliber automatic in it and two extra magazines. "It's loaded, Harry. Chamber a round as you leave camp."

Harry adjusted the belt, wrapped it around his waist, and buckled it as if he were a gunfighter.

He then handed one to Beth, who put it on and turned to Harry. "How do I look?" she asked.

Harry smiled. "Dangerous."

"Look for dry wood and tinder," Reggie instructed. "Stay close to camp, and please stay together. Once you got out of the Land Rover, you became part of the food chain. Keep your heads on a swivel and don't forget to look in the trees."

"We'll be careful," Beth said.

As they walked toward the outer perimeter of the camp, each pulled their pistol from the holster, chambered a round, and put them back in the holsters. For the first time, they felt a bit uneasy. They walked slowly, looking around like rabbits coming out of their holes, expecting to be pounced on. But as time passed, they relaxed. They went about gathering wood, talking and laughing, almost forgetting that they were deep in the wild and, as Reggie had put it, "part of the food chain."

They made several trips to the camp with arms full of firewood. On their last trip, Beth noticed something on the ground that snapped them back to reality. It was a depression in the sand about four inches in diameter, with four small depressions in an arc on one side. The entire depression was about six inches across. She stopped and stared. It was a lion track. Looking just ahead, there was another, then another. The stark reality of the situation turned her back into a rabbit and she froze in her tracks.

Harry, who hadn't noticed the tracks, turned toward her, his arms loaded with firewood. Seeing that she was startled, he too came back to reality. He looked at her and at the track at her feet. Then, realizing what was going on, he started looking around intently. He dropped the wood he was carrying, drew the .45 automatic from his belt, and took it off safety. They were close to camp, so the choice was simple: get back inside the camp!

Beth rushed to Harry's side and drew her weapon. Watching their perimeter, they hastened back to safety.

****

Sitting on a hill, camouflaged in the tall dry grass, a lion lay in the evening sun, watching the strangers travel in and out of his territory. It would have been easy to take the smaller one—she'd walked within a few yards of him. But he'd already fed and didn't hunt when he wasn't hungry. Besides, he would need to feed again tomorrow, and the intruder looked like it wasn't going anywhere. He decided to wait until they left the area to head back to the pride. He was an opportunistic hunter, he was an experienced hunter, and he would be hungry again. Why scare off tomorrow's dinner?

Lionesses normally brought food back to the pride, but he'd happened upon the herd of wildebeest and was able to take one of the young calves. After he watched the couple scurry out of his domain, he grabbed the remains of his meal in his teeth and headed back to the waiting pride. They would eat well tonight, and possibly tomorrow.

****

Arriving at the camp, Harry cleared and holstered his pistol, and they went over to Reggie.

"We found lion tracks out there," Beth said, shaken.

Reggie, focused intently on Beth as she spoke, asked, "How close to camp?"

Harry replied, "About a hundred yards or so along the ridge."

Reggie turned to Motaba and told him to arm up. He then told Harry and Beth to get into the tent and close it up while they checked the perimeter.

Reggie headed in the direction the couple indicated and found the tracks. He followed them to the spot where the lion had lain and watched them.

"Close," Motaba said, squatting over the blood spot where the dead wildebeest calf had lain.

Reggie, staring at the spot and looking back at where he'd seen the couple's boot prints, said, "Good thing the lion had fed. He could have taken them if he'd wanted to." Then he rose to his feet. "Let's get back to camp."

"Want to move camp?"

"No, the lion was passing through. We'll be careful."

"We got lucky," Motaba added.

"Yep."

Arriving back at camp, Reggie explained the situation to them. It was apparent the lion had fed before they entered the area. He told them it was also apparent that the lion had been watching them from the tall grass. "I told you that you'd entered the food chain. Now you see that I wasn't kidding. No one leaves the camp without Motaba or me, and no one leaves at night. Not for any reason. Understood?"

"Understood," they replied.

The four of them settled down around a fire and talked as they prepared a hot meal. Things were different now. The weapons were loaded all the time and were always within reach.

The bolt-action rifle Reggie carried leaned against the log next to him. There was a lot about Reggie that was rugged and old. His hat was weathered, his khakis were worn and tattered, and even his equipment showed signs of excessive wear, but the Remington 700 rifle and the .375 Holland & Holland magnum looked like they'd come out of the box moments ago. Their finishes were pristine, and the barrels were shiny with a thin coat of gun oil. A closer look revealed that they weren't leaning directly on the log, but against a small towel so there was no direct contact. Reggie knew what was important to survive and his weapons were at the top of the list. They would need those weapons tomorrow. They had found their prey, and the hunt was on.

The evening wore on and the couple went to bed. The days in the bush were hot, but the nights could get really cold. Harry and Beth zipped their sleeping bags together so they could spoon and keep each other warm. As Harry pulled her close to him, he could sense something was wrong.

"What's the matter, baby?" Harry asked.

"Nothin', hon," she lied.

"I can tell somethin's up. What is it?"

After a long tense pause, Beth replied, "I keep seeing that poor animal being butchered at the lodge. It was terrible."

"You know it isn't any different than what happens to cows to make a hamburger."

"Yeah, I know, but I never saw it before. It was like a horror movie. It'll take some getting used to."

"Don't think about it, baby. Try to get some sleep." He hugged her tightly.

"I know death is part of life. I just hate the thought of watching something suffer," she said.

"I understand, baby," Harry replied. "Are you ready to go home?"

"No," she replied as she squeezed the arm wrapped around her waist. "I'll be fine."

"OK. Goodnight, baby."

"Night," she said, trying to get the image out of her mind.

Harry felt Beth drift off to sleep in his arms, but what she'd said hit home in a way she couldn't imagine. If he were going to die from the tumor in his brain, would it be fair to put her through it? He decided not to dwell on it tonight. Tomorrow was going to be a busy day.

****

Harry looked through his binoculars at the kudu traveling down a game trail toward the watering hole in the valley. The last one in the herd was the biggest. Harry's heart raced as he watched them. The animals looked like they were in a zoo. They were very skittish and constantly aware of their surroundings as they headed toward the watering hole at the base of the valley.

Reggie was looking through his binoculars as well. He and Harry talked quietly as they followed the unsuspecting animals. "The last one is your trophy," he said quietly. "But it's too far away."

"How far would you say?" Harry asked.

"Eight hundred meters or so…. We'll have to creep up on him."

Beth looked at the little specs without binoculars. She preferred it that way. She didn't want to look into the eyes of the animal that was about to be murdered. She didn't want to ruin the trip for Harry, but she didn't want it ruined for her either. She decided to try to suppress her anxieties and go along for the ride.

Motaba remained back at camp. He would be joining them with the land rover if and when they made a kill.

When the small herd was far enough down the game trail, Reggie signaled for them to follow. The three of them—Reggie, Harry and Beth—began a slow trek along the trail after the herd. "They'll be headed back the way they came. We need to be within range when they do."

"You sure they'll go back the same way?" Harry questioned.

"Nothing is definite, but if they don't get spooked, they don't sense us, and no predator gets in the mix, they should. When they do, we need to be in position, downwind, quiet, camouflaged, and ready," Reggie explained.

They began an incredibly slow but deliberate creep toward the well-used game trail. Each footstep made noise, and they took efforts to minimize that unnatural sound. The creaking of leather and crushing of dry grass under their feet seemed to cry out that a human predator was on the prowl. They took a dozen or so steps and stopped to glass the valley, a dozen more steps and glassed again.

Beth was at the back of the trio and just followed along. After an hour, they came within about one hundred meters of the trail. Trees shaded them and tall grass concealed them from approaching prey.

Reggie had led them into position like a true predator. Little did he know that another predator had the same plan.

****

Hidden in the tall grass, six hundred pounds of muscle and teeth watched silently as the three strangers slid into position in front of him, his breathing shallow and quiet. He was hungry, but patient. He looked at the three and decided he would take the last one. It was the smallest and would be the easiest to catch and kill. Experience had taught him that whenever he prepared to strike, the prey would scatter and leave the weakest to fend for themselves. It was survival of the fittest.

He watched and waited as they settled down in the grass. He breathed deeply, filling his blood with extra oxygen, giving him strength for the pursuit that was about to come. His muscles tensed. His jewel-like eyes locked on his target, so frail, so tender and juicy. He would feast soon. His breathing became deeper, and he felt his blood racing. He was a loaded spring about to release.

****

Reggie was looking through his binoculars as the herd approached their position. “Get ready,” he whispered. He was so focused on the herd he didn’t hear the strange breathing nearby.

Harry, on the other hand, did catch the subtle hint of impending danger, although he didn’t know what it was. The hair on the back of his neck stood up. He turned to Beth who didn’t want to be a party to the slaughter. She sat about ten feet behind them, quiet and out of the way. To Harry’s horror and disbelief, he saw movement and two jewel-like eyes through the tall grass behind Beth. The head of a lion burst through the grass, and the animal was in a full run toward Beth. Harry instinctively spun around and put the rifle on the huge beast. He didn’t take time to aim. There wasn’t time. He stroked the trigger, and the report from the .375 H&H magnum was deafening.

Reggie immediately turned around to see what was happening, but his rifle was not in his hands and he was unable to help. Harry watched helplessly as the lion pounced on Beth, and she screamed in horror.

The fear, the shock, the terror as he saw the head and front paws of the beast completely cover her was more than Harry could stand. He knew that another shot was impossible without hitting Beth. Instantly, he was on his feet and he pounced on the huge lion. He had his knife in his hand and was ready for the fight of his life, but to his surprise, the lion didn't put one up. He grabbed the lion's mane and pulled the head toward him to look at the lifeless eyes of the beast. Seeing blood on Beth, Harry's heart sank. He felt so helpless. He wondered how he would get her medical attention. He wiped the blood away as she struggled beneath the monster, looking for the worst injuries, but other than a few cuts and scratches, none were to be found.

"Get it off me, Harry!" Beth screamed, still in shock from the sudden attack. "Get it off!"

Reggie was there in an instant, and the two of them pulled the former King of the Jungle off Beth as she struggled to her feet. Her face, neck, and chest were covered in blood, as was her hair. She ran around in a blind panic as the two looked on. Harry was in utter disbelief at what had just happened, but Beth seemed to be OK, and now the whole thing seemed a bit funny.

Maybe it was the adrenalin, or maybe it was just the sight of her covered in blood, or maybe it was a little of both, but for whatever reason, Harry and Reggie looked at each other and started to laugh.

"Well, I'm glad you two find this so amusing!" she bellowed. At first, she seemed truly pissed that they found this whole thing funny, all the while protesting that it wasn't funny at all. "Look at my hair! It's gonna be like a brown helmet by the time we get back to camp." Then, amazingly, she started to laugh with them. They laughed together for a couple of minutes then they settled down and got back to reality.

Reggie said, "You have your kill, Harry," as he pulled up the massive front paw to reveal an entry wound under the neck. "The round went through him like a freight train, killed him instantly."

All the blood on Beth was from the lion. Things had worked out. The quick, instinctive shot had found its mark. Beth was safe, he had a trophy she would not be upset about, and he felt like a hero.

Beth began to wipe away the blood. She was still shaking but had managed to gather her wits. She walked over to her pack and opened it. Rummaging around, she pulled out the camera. Harry and Reggie smiled as she motioned for them to move over next to the beast.

"OK, mister big game, pose for the camera," she said.

Harry grabbed his rifle and fedora and settled on one knee behind the lion, holding the rifle with the butt on the ground and barrel in the air, his chest puffed out, and a smile on his face.

Beth snapped several pictures as he changed positions. Then Reggie came over to take the camera from her.

"You get in there, too. After all, you lured him in," Reggie said.

Beth rushed over, and the two knelt together with the downed lion as Reggie took pictures.

As the story was told, Motaba had heard the gunshot and figured Harry had made his kill. He picked up his two-way radio and waited for instructions. It wasn't long before he'd heard Reggie call him. He was told where to meet them and that they had indeed made a kill. He arrived in the Land Rover and stopped in his tracks as he saw the dead lion.

"Nice kill," Motaba muttered as he approached, drawing his knife. Then he and Reggie began to field dress the beast.

This was the part that had disturbed Beth back at the lodge, but this time it didn't bother her. She wondered if it was because she'd seen it done before or because the lion had tried to kill her. She didn't know, but she did know that Harry had saved her life. There was no doubt about that. He was her hero.

The four wrestled the now lighter lion into the back of the Land Rover and headed back to camp. It was still early in the day, and they decided not to stay in camp another night. The safety and luxury of the lodge was preferable after the events of the day. The tents were broken down and packed away, the site was policed, and the trailer was packed.

Harry leaned against the corner of the Land Rover with Beth snuggled up beside him. He adored her, and he'd almost gotten her killed. He and his quest to find himself had almost destroyed the one great thing in his life. The scene kept running through his mind. He could see the lion pouncing on Beth over and over, but with different results. Every time that image played out in his head, he felt sick to his stomach and realized how lucky he was that she was alive. And lucky was the word. He didn't even remember taking the shot. He couldn't even be sure it was a shot and not an accidental discharge. What if he'd hit Beth? How could he have lived with that? The bullet must have gone right by her head. He decided to put it out of his mind. It was enough that they were safe and headed back to civilization. Harry drifted off to sleep as the Land Rover bounced along the road.

They arrived at the lodge late that night. It had been a long day, and Beth went straight up to their room. Harry went to oversee the skinning of his lion. He hoped no one would know that it had been a panic shot; he'd like them to think he'd deliberately shot the animal. He wondered how to tell the story.

When he got to the shack, Motaba was hooking the lion up to the hoist. It didn't look as big as it did when it was draped across Beth, at least until they hoisted it up. Stretched out, it was massive. The mane was full and its fur, though showing signs of living in the brush, was in excellent condition.

Motaba asked, "Do you want to have a rug made from the skin, or do you want it mounted?"

Harry thought for a second of the one in their suite. "I want it mounted!"

He then noticed a young couple watching from the other side of the shack. It occurred to him that a few days ago, that had been him and Beth, standing in about the same spot, as the kudu was being skinned. He saw the look of excitement on the man's face and the overwhelmed look on the woman's. Then he realized he was standing in about the same spot as the hunter who had killed the kudu on that day and, as fate would have it, Reggie walked over and stood beside him with a drink in his hand.

The circle is complete, Harry thought.

A few of the other hunters came over to congratulate Harry on such a fine kill. This was what he was afraid of. He knew they were expecting a story of how he'd tracked the beast and taken a long shot, compensating for wind and distance, and how the beast had charged at the last moment, forcing him to think quickly. The truth was that it had been an accidental discharge with fortunate results, and he'd almost killed Beth in the process, but these fears were soon put to rest as Reggie came to the rescue. Reggie intercepted the attention of the hunters and introduced them to Harry.

"Gentlemen, have you met Harry? This is his kill."

"Nice to meet you, Harry," one gentleman said.

"Excellent kill, Harry," another said with respect.

"Thank you," Harry said, shaking their hands.

Reggie, sensing Harry's lack of confidence, took control of the conversation. "It was amazing. We'd just eased into a blind, about to take a nice kudu, when this lion burst out of the tall grass. It was headed straight for us. Harry spun around and took him out with one shot." Reggie went on with his story, laying it on thicker and heavier as he went, as the two hunters smiled and nodded. He made Harry look like a seasoned hunter instead of a rookie who'd gotten lucky.

Motaba made quick work of the lion, and before long, it was no more than a head with salted fur on its way to the taxidermist, and a bunch of steaks.

Harry went back to the lodge, showered, and joined Beth in bed. She'd been sound asleep, but responded as soon as he got into bed. She rolled over and pulled herself close to him.

"Are you all right, baby?" he asked.

"It all happened so fast," Beth replied, still half asleep. "It just occurred to me that I was almost killed."

"I know. Life can turn on a dime."

"Thank God, you were there to protect me."

Harry squeezed her tightly. "You ready to go home?"

"Yeah, it's time," she said, snuggling up to his massive chest.

"'Night, baby," he whispered as he kissed her forehead.

"'Night."

Chapter Sixteen

The next day, they were on a plane headed home. The vacation had recharged them, but had taken a lot out of them as well. Harry felt the pressures of his job creeping back up on him as he began to restart the parts of his brain that had been dormant while on the trip. They hadn't used all of his vacation, but he was ready to go home. And there was a lot to do. He had to get to a doctor to do battle with the tumor in his head. When he'd beaten it, he would ask Beth to marry him.

He wondered, "What did I learn? Who am I? Did it really matter?" He now knew that there was a world out there he hadn't realized existed. He also knew there was more to life than work and money. There were adventure and excitement, challenges and experiences, and, yes, love. He had photos and the lion as a trophy, but more importantly he had the experiences, which had helped him grow, live, and partake of the world and what it had to offer. Now was the time to get to work.

****

The journey was over, and Harry and Beth were happy to be home. Jetlag hit them again, and correcting their sleeping habits would take some time.

Beth stirred from her sound sleep, feeling good to be in Harry's apartment. It had been a fantastic vacation, the best she'd ever had, but it was over. And she was ready for it to be over, ready to get back into her life. She rolled over to find

Harry gone. He was in the kitchen with the morning paper and a cup of coffee.

Harry was also ready to get back to life. He'd been up for over an hour by this time and was ready to get going. He had a long list of things to do, a mountain of mail to sort through, preparations to make for work, and of course, a trip to the doctor. It was strange that he put them in that order, but that was how he saw it. Get the little things out of the way first and then focus on the biggest challenge.

He smiled as Beth entered the kitchen with the thick blanket wrapped around her, a terrible case of bed hair, and a still-asleep look on her face. She shuffled over and kissed him on the cheek, to which he responded, "Morning, Sunshine."

She managed "Mmrrrnng" through sleepy lips and poured herself a cup of coffee. She came back to the table and sat down next to Harry.

"What's on your agenda today?" Harry asked, looking over the paper.

"Back to work…hopefully go back to work," she replied, somewhat unconcerned. "It shouldn't be a problem. How about you?"

There was the carefree attitude Harry loved about her. "Just getting my bearings," Harry said as he turned his attention back to the paper. His stocks were doing well. His head was getting back into the game. He still was technically on vacation, but the suspense was getting to him. He wanted to talk to Stan. He'd been on a journey and learned a lot about himself. He wasn't sure if what he'd learned was what Stan was looking for, but it didn't really matter. It was what it was.

"I have to attend to things at the office, babe," he told Beth. "You need me to drop you off anywhere?"

"No, I think I'm gonna lounge around for a while. Have a great day," she said. It was as if they were already married, they were so comfortable with each other.

Harry climbed into the Mercedes for the first time in a long time and sighed in relief when it started after having sat for so long. He drove to the office to find his parking space was no longer his. He wondered momentarily if he'd been replaced while he was away. Then he realized he was returning to a new position that would have a new parking space. He drove to the next floor of the garage—the floor reserved for the top executives—and found an empty spot with his name stenciled above it. It began to sink in. He'd made it. He was one of the elite. He had a loose grip on the bottom rung of the next ladder. He pulled into the spot and headed inside.

Arriving at Stan's office, he walked up to Heather's desk. There she was, just the way she was the last time he was there. The pictures of her family were in the same place on the desk, but this time things seemed different. He could see how she could be with her husband. He could see past the ordinary man and into his eyes, as well as into hers. Harry had changed. His feelings for Beth had awakened a new Harry, one who knew there are better things than money and power.

"Hello, Harry. Welcome back!" Heather said, standing to greet him. "Did you have a nice vacation?"

"It was eventful," Harry responded. "Is Mr. Jacobson available?"

"Let me check," she replied, picking up the phone to buzz his line. "Mr. Jacobson, Mr. Stevenson is here to see you." After a brief pause, she said, "Yes, sir," and hung up. "He's busy for the next few minutes, but he wants me to show you to your new office."

"Lead the way," Harry said, following her into the hall. They stopped at a door that didn't yet have a name on it. She opened it and they stepped inside. There he found a small and somewhat cramped office that, for a second, he thought was his. Then he realized it would be his secretary's office. He followed Heather to the large, inner office that was in the process of being remodeled. Harry's feelings of having been replaced were gone now; he was feeling like royalty. A huge rounded desk was in the center of the room, close to the window. The room smelled of paint and new carpeting. Ladders and drop cloths were strewn about. Heather stood off to the side and watched as Harry walked around the room to the far side of the desk and stared out the window. He was in the office for only a few minutes when he heard a familiar voice behind him.

"We didn't expect you back for a few more weeks," Harry heard from the doorway. There stood Stan Jacobson, smiling. "So, Harry, what do you think?"

"Beautiful," Harry replied, looking around. "I'm not back yet; I just wanted to see if I still work here," he said with levity.

"You still work here, all right. So, did you learn anything?" Stan asked.

"I did. More than I can put into words. There's a whole world out there, and it would be criminal to miss it."

Stan's smiled again. "You figured it out, didn't you?"

"I think I did."

"Good, I knew you would. Now go on and enjoy the rest of your time off. Don't worry, we'll hold down the fort until you get back. Then you can tell me all about it."

Harry shook his hand and walked out of his new office with a renewed feeling of being needed. And it was good.

Back in his car, Harry headed to the doctor. He began to think about the situation seriously for the first time. He hadn't allowed himself to think about the possibility that the tumor would kill him. He had options. But what if this was the end? And what about Beth?

"Stop it!" he said out loud, then thought, *I'm getting ahead of myself.*

Harry drove to the doctor's by instinct alone. His mind was on other things. He made his way up to the office, his files from the Cayman Islands in hand, in plenty of time for his appointment. Then sitting in the lobby, he had a premonition. This wasn't going to turn out well.

Doctor Richardson was Harry's primary care physician. He had a great manner, and Harry liked him. Surely he would give Harry some good news. He studied the reports and images in Harry's file for what seemed like an eternity. As he paged back and forth, the corners of his mouth sagged. The prognosis was obvious to Dr. Richardson, but it wasn't his burden to tell Harry.

Seeing the expression on the doctor's face, Harry began to panic. "Talk to me," he pleaded.

"Excuse me for a minute, Harry," he said. He walked out of the room, taking Harry's file with him. He was gone for another eternity, and he walked back in and sat at his desk.

"Harry, you need to see a specialist. He can tell you more about this," he said, starting to write. "I've called him, and he's expecting you this afternoon."

"Should I bother?" Harry asked.

Dr. Richardson sat back in his chair, removed his glasses, and chose his words carefully. "Harry, it doesn't look good, but this isn't my specialty. That's why I'm referring you. Let's take this one step at a time."

Harry felt his heart sink as he took the referral and his file. He could sense Dr. Richardson's hopelessness. He thanked the doctor and walked out of the office.

Dr. Richardson hated this part of being a doctor. It was never easy to tell a patient there was no hope, and he felt a rush of guilt for passing the buck to his colleague. He'd been seeing Harry for many years. Would it have been better for Harry to hear it from him? Then he stopped to call his wife and daughter, just to tell them that he loved them. *"But for the grace of God, there go I,"* he thought as he dialed.

It was late in the evening when Harry arrived back at his apartment. Beth was there and excited to see him. He tried to put on his best game face, especially since she was so excited, like a kid at Christmas for some reason. But he wasn't in the mood to be sociable.

The appointment had not gone as he had hoped. The years that he'd hoped for turned out to be months. There was no hope. There was one treatment that might extend his life for a few months, but it would ruin his quality of life. No matter what, he would deteriorate and die. The headaches and the tiredness had been symptoms, but the way the tumor had developed excluded surgical treatment. Now it was so advanced that he was done for. The only question was what to do now.

Harry withdrew into himself. He was feeling hopeless and helpless, asking God why this had to happen to him now. Beth, not knowing what was wrong, didn't know how to help him. She'd never seen him like this. He was still kind and courteous, but not the same Harry. She decided to let it ride and wait for him to tell her what was wrong.

Harry started searching for other options on the Internet. He looked up the type of tumor he had, hoping to find some type of radical treatment. All his efforts led to one name—Doctor Grace Young, but she was listed as a spiritual healer. He dismissed her and kept moving on. But after seeing her name mentioned many times, and noticing she was in nearby Clearwater, he decided to look her up. What could it hurt?

He called Dr. Richardson and asked if he'd heard of her. He said that he had, although he had no experience with her. Then said the same thing Harry had thought, "What could it hurt?"

Harry contacted Dr. Young and found out she wasn't seeing patients, but he let her know he was desperate. It sounded as though she'd given up her practice. But after she'd talked with him for a while, she agreed to see him the next day.

Harry arrived at her modest office and was greeted by the doctor herself. There was no staff, no secretary, and no grand office. Instead, he found her to be a simple woman, soft-spoken and down to earth. She led Harry to a comfortable den, offered him a seat, and asked if he would like coffee. He graciously accepted. She left for a moment and returned with a tray holding coffee, cream, and sweetener. She poured him a cup and sat back with her own.

"How can I help you, Harry? Do you mind if I call you Harry?"

"That's fine, Dr. Young," Harry began.

"Please, call me Grace," she interrupted.

"OK, Grace. I found you on the Internet. To tell you the truth, I don't know why I'm here, except that I don't know where else to turn. Everyone I've talked to has told me my life is over, and I'm not ready for that. I am looking for a doctor who can help me fix this thing in my head. Money is no object. I can't help but think there's someone out there who has the answer, someone who has some kind of treatment that can help me." Harry's eyes teared. He felt the panic he'd been pushing back since he learned of his condition.

"Harry, calm down," Grace said. "I believe I can help you, but I don't think it's the kind of help that you're looking for."

"What do you mean, Grace?" Harry asked. "What kind of help?"

"Let's not get ahead of ourselves," she replied, opening a desk drawer. She pulled out a patient release form and gave it to Harry. "This is a HIPAA release that will allow me to talk to your doctors. Let's take it one step at a time, OK?"

Harry took the form, filled it out, and handed it back to her.

"Everything is going to be all right, Harry," she said reassuringly. "Now go home and try to relax. I'll call you after I've spoken with your doctors."

Harry composed himself and stood. To his surprise, Grace came over and hugged him. "Don't worry," she said. "I'll try to help you."

Harry left the office feeling differently than he had when he arrived. He didn't know what she thought she could do that other doctors couldn't. There was no talk of surgery, radiation, chemotherapy, or other medications, but at this point, he was willing to take any help he could get. She radiated an inner peace that comforted and relaxed Harry. He wanted to come back, and he would. She was the first doctor who said she could help him. She was his only hope.

On his way home, he saw a familiar raggedy man on the corner, William Holt. It seemed like forever since he'd seen him.

William appeared to recognize Harry and his shiny Mercedes. He started to walk away, but he turned around after a few steps. Harry leaned out the window and Bill walked over, taking the twenty-dollar bill Harry held out to him.

"Thanks, Harry," he said, turning away.

"Take care, Bill," Harry said so quietly that Bill never heard him. He wished that there was something that he could do for Bill. He'd seen something in Bill's eyes that pleaded for help, but what could he do? He was a dying financial officer, not a lawyer.

That evening, Harry got a call from Grace. She wanted him to come in the next day. He agreed and was reassured by her voice.

Beth had gotten her job back at The Boiling Point. After all, she was the hottest waitress they had. Harry almost told her not to bother; he made enough money to take care of her. But he needed some time to himself, and her job took her out of the apartment for long periods of time. He loved her, but he wasn't ready to tell her about his condition yet. He didn't know if he should. He'd seen people with cancer. He knew how they got when the pain took over. And with a brain tumor, his mind would go. He didn't want her to see him like that. He never wanted to see a look of pity for him on her face. He didn't want to see her suffer with him in his final days. He decided that when that time came, he would do something about it. But for now, he loved her too much to let her go.

They went out to dinner that night. Beth kept feeling that Harry was different, but couldn't put her finger on what it was. He was preoccupied all the time, and there were phone calls, calls he left the room to take. Was there another woman? Had she ruined their vacation? She was so sure he was going to ask her to marry him, but he hadn't. She loved him with all her heart and didn't want to lose him, but she didn't know what to do. She called her mother for advice, telling her all about Harry. Her mother said, "Let it ride. Men are complicated." So that's what she decided to do. Let it ride.

They enjoyed a nice dinner together. They were cordial, but there was a heavy presence at the table with them that they both tried to ignore. It was obvious that something was wrong; Beth couldn't let it ride any longer.

"Do you still love me, Harry?" she blurted.

Harry was caught completely off guard. He looked into her face and felt the overwhelming passion for her he'd set aside since learning of his diagnosis. He didn't know what to say. He loved her, but wondered if he should fight for her when his end was so near. This was an opportunity to end the relationship. If he didn't, he'd be reassuring her only to let her down later.

"Baby, why do you ask? Of course, I love you." That was no lie. He loved her more than life itself.

"You've been distant lately," she explained. "Not the same old Harry"

"Are you calling me old?" he asked, smiling.

She smiled back and relaxed a little with the humor. "You know what I mean."

"I'm sorry, baby. I just have a lot on my mind," he said, trying to reassure her.

"I thought there might be another woman," she said, a little shyly.

Harry looked at her and smiled again. "There could never be another woman. In my world, the sun rises and sets on you."

She felt relieved, and the worried look faded from her face. He did love her. He'd never lied to her. She was sure of it. She decided to take her mother's advice.

Chapter Seventeen

Harry arrived at Dr. Young's office for his next appointment. It looked a little different. Things were missing from the shelves and walls, and boxes were lying around. Grace took him into the same room they'd met in before and brought in coffee without asking. They sat down together.

Harry didn't know what to expect and was a bit apprehensive. Once they were settled, Grace began.

"Harry, tell me about your life."

Harry was reminded of the meeting in Stan's office months ago, but this time he had more to say.

"Well, I have a beautiful girlfriend. She is the light of my life. We've been together for several months now and just got back from a wonderful vacation. I want to ask her to marry me, but that doesn't seem fair now." He paused, for a moment. "I just received a huge promotion at work, one I've been working all my life to get, making more money than I ever imagined. I am, to a degree, independently wealthy. I have a nice apartment, a nice car…and let me see, oh yea, only a few months to live."

"Have you lived a good life, Harry? Have you made a difference in the lives of others?"

"I'd like to think so…I don't know."

"I have talked to your doctors. I know what you're dealing with," she said calmly.

"I don't know where to turn," Harry said, the tears welling up in his eyes again.

"Harry, I think I can help you, but not in the way that you think," she said quietly and soothingly.

Harry felt a glimmer of hope as he heard the soothing words. "How?"

"Harry, it's time to look at what is possible and what is not. There are things you can do, and there are things you can't. You must focus your energy on those that you can."

Harry didn't want to give up. He wanted to fight. He wanted to live.

"There is nothing you can do to save your life, Harry, but you can decide to live it. Don't waste time trying to save it. Use the time to live it. Make an effort to make every minute count. You're still in pretty good health, but that won't last. Don't waste the time you have."

"I don't want to die!" Harry pleaded.

"We are all going to die, Harry…you, me, everyone. That is a certainty. Some people live to a grand old age, some die as children. Some do things in their life, some waste their time. If there was anything that might save your life, I would say that you should do it. But it is time to make a decision. Use the time or lose the time."

Harry listened as she went on. At first he was angry, then he began to understand, and finally, as he began to accept what the limitations of his situation were, a sense of peace came over him. She was right.

"There is only one thing of value in the entire world, Harry. Do you know what that one thing is?"

"Family?" he guessed.

"No. not family," she responded.

"Your health?"

"No. Harry, it's not health. It's time! We have only so much of it. No matter how rich we are, we can't buy it. No matter how powerful we are, we can't demand it. You can't steal, borrow it, create it, bargain with it, or control it. All you can do is use it or waste it, and when it's gone, it's gone. The only question now is how you want to spend it. You can waste it being bitter or selfish, or you can enjoy the time you have to the fullest. You can make your life mean something. You can live on through the lives of others. You can make a difference in the lives of those who would otherwise have no hope. It's your life. Time is a treasure."

Harry was both listening to her and evaluating his personal situation. When she stopped, he returned from his reverie.

"Well, Harry, how are you going to spend it?"

Harry felt acceptance envelop him, and his muscles relaxed. He realized what she was trying to tell him, and it gave him peace. He would no longer have to fight the daily fight, the mentally demanding war he had always fought. He could do what's right for his fellow man and make a difference in their lives. With this epiphany, his expression softened and he stared directly into her eyes. He found words slowly and spoke them with surrender. He submitted to the inevitable; there was nothing else he could do.

"I understand," he said. "I'm not going to waste the treasure of time."

Harry felt as if a new chapter in his life had opened—the final chapter. Knowing that his life was finite, he wanted the rest of it to count for something. There was no reason to work anymore. He had plenty of money. He wanted to spend as much time enjoying every moment he had left, but he also wanted to make a difference.

He decided to spend as much quality time as he could with Beth, and when he began to deteriorate, he would send her away. She would hate him for it, but he didn't want her to watch him suffer. He loved her too much. He would rather have her upset than to suffer along with him, watching him die.

There were others he wanted to help. Those who had nowhere else to turn—like William Holt. But he would need some assistance. He decided the first thing on the agenda was to leave his job.

He went to work and straight to his new office. He sat at his new desk and looked over the room. He imagined what it would have been like to deal with the hectic life of an executive in this new arena. He thought of what he could accomplish with the power that he would wield in the new position. He imagined the phone ringing in the outer office, and his secretary buzzing his intercom to tell him someone urgently needed to talk to him. All the power that he once craved now seemed utterly unimportant.

Stan Jacobson walked down the corridor toward his office and paused when he saw Harry's door open. Harry wasn't due back for a few days, and he smiled at the thought of him being so anxious to return. He walked into the outer office and, seeing Harry sitting at the desk, knocked on the open door.

Harry turned his chair around to see Stan at the door. "Please, come in. You're just the man I need to see," he said standing up.

"Please, Harry, this is your office," Stan said as he entered the room, motioning for him to keep his seat. He walked over to the visitor's side of the desk and sat down. "You ready to come back?"

Harry reached into his briefcase, took out a letter of resignation, and handed it to Stan.

"What's this?" Stan asked as he opened the letter and began to read it. The letter began with his medical condition and ended with his resignation. He'd rewritten it a few times before he got it the way he wanted it. Stan finished the letter and refolded it. He sat, silent, then looked directly at Harry. "Harry, I'm so sorry. Are you sure nothing can be done?"

"I'm sure," he replied, emotionless.

"What can I do for you?" Stan offered.

"I'm glad you asked. There is something I need."

"If it is within my power, it's yours," Stan said, anxious to help.

"First, I have a lot of unfinished business to deal with. I need to use this office until I complete it. Is that possible?"

"Of course," Stan replied.

"Second, no one, and I mean no one, is to know about this until I'm gone. It'll make it too hard to get anything done."

"No problem."

"And finally, I need access to the firm's legal team. At my expense, of course."

"At your disposal. May I ask, what are you're working on?"

"Just going to right a few wrongs. One in particular."

"OK, Harry. You want to start right away, I assume. Your secretary will be here Monday morning."

"My secretary?" he asked.

"I see no reason to stop her from coming. She'll be necessary to keep the illusion, and you'll need her at your disposal. Is there anything else?"

"There is. Do we have a detective on staff?" Harry asked.

Chapter Eighteen

The morning dew was cold and wet. Bill Holt had found a spot to sleep behind an all-night laundry. There was a space between the building and a dumpster where the exhaust from the dryers kept him warm. It was almost like torture—warm when they were running, cold when they shut off, but at least he had the intermittent warmth to help him through the night. The rising sun warmed things, but the night of inactivity and restless sleep, combined with his dew-soaked clothes, chilled him to the bone. He preferred to sleep, but hunger dictated that he start his morning routine.

He rolled out of the newspapers and filth, stood up and walked away from his sleeping spot, and began to relieve himself against a wall across the alley. As he did, he felt he was being watched. The police didn't bother him as long as he kept to himself; he thought someone might want to take one of his few possessions. He felt his body tense, preparing to do battle. He zipped up his pants and quickly turned to face—a well-dressed man standing a few feet away. He was not what Bill expected. He slowly relaxed as he realized he wasn't in danger.

"William Holt?" the man asked.

Bill felt at a disadvantage. He was comfortable around homeless people, but didn't like being around others. "Who wants to know?"

"We have a mutual friend," he said.

"Yeah. I don't have any friends," Bill retorted.

"You're wrong. You have a good friend, and he sent me to find you."

"Really? Who's that?" Bill inquired.

"Harry Stevenson."

He remembered Harry. And he remembered how he dredged up all the misery he was hiding from. "Yeah, I know Harry. Who are you?"

"The name's Leo. I'm a PI hired by Harry. You hungry?"

"Always," Bill replied.

"Come with me," the stranger said, starting to turn away.

Bill stood where he was, looking at Leo with confusion. "What for?" he asked.

"We need to get you cleaned up and get you some chow. We have a big day ahead."

Not knowing what to make of this stranger, Bill did not move.

"Look, have you got someplace better to be right now?" Leo asked.

Without a word, Bill followed Leo out of the alley and down the block. Leo Mason was a big man, six-foot-two and two hundred seventy-five pounds, with broad shoulders, a narrow waist, and a purposeful walk. His voice demanded compliance.

The word "chow" had given Bill a clue. "When were you in?" Bill asked.

"I was discharged five years ago," Leo said.

"I was a Marine, too."

"I know, Bill. That's why I'm here." He led Bill to a motel, where he rented a room. Looking Bill up-and-down, he said, "I'm gonna guess you wear about a thirty-six waist. That about right, Bill?"

"Yeah, that's about right." He hadn't worn a pair of pants he didn't find in the garbage for so long that the question seemed strange.

"You go get cleaned up, and I'm gonna get you some clean clothes. What size shoes?"

"Twelve." It reminded him of boot camp.

"OK, I'll be back in a few. Get cleaned up."

Bill took the key Leo handed him and went into the modest motel room. He felt funny about the whole situation. He locked and bolted the door. It was the first time he'd felt secure since before he ended up on the streets. Looking around the room, he felt out of place. He wanted to take a hot shower. Making sure the door was locked, he stripped off his filthy clothing and climbed into the shower. The hot water felt like heaven. He couldn't remember the last time he'd had a hot shower. He smiled as he washed away the dirt and grime he'd been living with for so long.

When the hot water was gone, he got out and dried off. Lying down on the bed, he picked up the remote, and turned on the TV. He thought about all the modern conveniences he'd missed these last few years, how low he'd sunk, and a wave of sadness overtook him. Just about then, there was a knock on the door. He got up to answer it and realized even that was strange. When he opened the door, Leo came in and set some bags on the bed. He handed Bill a brand new pair of jeans, a t-shirt, socks, and underwear. Then he set a new pair of tennis shoes on the floor. Bill felt as if he were dreaming.

"Get dressed, Bill. We have a lot to do," Leo said.

Bill looked at the clothes he'd been wearing, then took out his personal possessions and put the clothes in the bag to be thrown away. Goodbye and good riddance.

By midday, Bill had been to a barber and a restaurant, and was feeling like a new man. His hair was cut, his beard was gone and, for the first time in years, he didn't smell. Now it was time to get to work. Leo took Bill to his office and they sat down at his desk. He picked up his phone, hit a few buttons, and said, "Yes, sir, he's here now." Leo took out a legal pad and a pen, saying to Bill, "I heard about what happened. Now I need to hear it from you, and don't leave anything out. Anything. Understand?"

"I've been through this," Bill said, "What good can it do?"

"It's different this time, Bill," Leo said as Harry entered and sat down beside Bill. "This time you have money and power on your side."

Chapter Nineteen

Tyler sat in the salon of *Dividends* with his bags packed. He was waiting for the letter telling him that he was out of a job. Maria had left a few days before, and it had been an emotional goodbye. He hated her being gone; he didn't like change. Now he sat in the quiet boat, missing his friend, uncertain of his future, going through his mail. He came to a letter addressed to him. It was from the company, and it was what he dreaded.

He looked at it for a minute before opening it. He felt the same sinking feeling he'd felt watching Maria walk away for the last time. They said they'd stay in touch and wouldn't forget each other, but those were lies. They both knew that fate would dictate their course and that the new heading would lead them forever apart. That was the way of things. And now here was this letter. Opening it, he was surprised to see it was from Harry.

Dear Tyler,

I want to thank you for the great vacation. Beth and I enjoyed ourselves. You were a hero, rescuing Capt. Sanchez during the storm. You are cool under pressure and skilled on the water. You know that boat inside and out, and you treat it like your own. These are the traits of a great captain and what I brought before the board of directors.

They were less than enthusiastic about putting *Dividends* in the hands of a captain your age, but after they heard of the plight we faced that morning, your courage and skill convinced them that you are the only man for the job. So the job is yours, if you want it.

There is no need to thank me; you earned it. If you're willing, review and sign the attached contract, then send it back in the enclosed envelope. It's up to you, Tyler. Don't let me down.

Your friend,

Harry Stevenson

Tyler pulled out the contract with disbelief. He'd had his captain's license for a while, but now he had the opportunity to be in charge of the finest sportfish in the marina. As soon as the other captains heard Maria was leaving, they began bombarding the owners with applications. And now it was his for the taking.

Tyler looked the contract over, took out a pen, scribbled his name, and headed for the post office. His mood was lighter. His home was secure. The boat was now his to command. He still felt his life had taken a different course, but now it was toward calm seas, and he was excited about it. He'd learned a lot from Maria, and he'd put it to good use. There was only one thing to say, the only thing he could say: "Thanks, Harry."

Chapter Twenty

André walked into his shop after stopping to get the mail. His business was struggling; the economic downturn had really hurt him. He'd lost most of his retirement and used what was left to subsidize his business. He was waiting for things to pick up, so he could stop the financial hemorrhaging. The business still had a modest income, but not enough to pay his mortgage on the building and keep up with expenses. He walked through the dive shop to his office, checking through the morning mail; a dive magazine, a couple of dive certifications, a stack of bills, yes… of course, more bills, and an official-looking letter from his bank. *Oh man, that can't be good news,* he thought. *I'll leave it for last.* And there was a letter from H. Stevenson. "Harry," he said out loud, opening it first.

> Dear André,
>
> Beth and I want to thank you for being a part of the best vacation that we ever had. You are a fantastic instructor and a good man. We're including some of the pictures that we took on the dive with you. They might look good on your wall.
>
> I know that things are tough for you right now, so I made a few calls. You'll be getting a dive magazine soon. Take a look at the ad on page ten. I think it might help in these slow times.

André put down the letter and went back to the day's mail and the magazine. He hadn't noticed that it was one he didn't subscribe to. He flipped immediately to page ten and couldn't believe his eyes. There he was, in a full-color, full-page ad, with Harry and Beth. The pictures were from the wreck dive, and the ad was obviously professionally done. He stared for a moment, and then went back to Harry's letter.

> The ad is paid for a full year in advance. You can change it any time you want.
>
> Also, you should soon be getting a letter from your bank. Open it right away. It will help. We want to thank you again for the fantastic experience, not to mention saving my life.
>
> Sincerely,
>
> Harry

André went back to the mail again and took out the letter from the bank. He opened it and began to read. It was a release of lien on his shop! Harry had paid off his mortgage. André felt a surge of relief as he realized he could make it now that there were no more monthly mortgage payments. He could go back to enjoying every day as he had in the beginning. "Thank you, Harry," he muttered. "You saved my life, too!"

Suddenly the morning quiet was interrupted by the ringing of the phone. André turned around in his chair to answer it. "André's Dive Shop…, yes…, yes, that's right…, I can schedule you that week…. I just need some information… "

As he talked, he looked at the answering machine. He had nine messages waiting. "Thanks again, Harry."

Chapter Twenty-one

Reggie found a delivery truck pulled up to the front of the hunting lodge. The driver brought down the power-lift gate with a large crate on it. He had Reggie sign for the package and wheeled the crate into the lodge.

Not knowing what it was, Reggie pulled off the packing slip and found it was from a taxidermist. He wasn't expecting anything, but he went to the tool shed for a pry bar so he could see what was inside. Motaba, seeing Reggie with the tool, followed him. They opened the crate to find a fully mounted adult lion in a standing position with mouth open and teeth exposed. It was of exceptional quality and would make a great addition to the trophy room. A letter was attached.

> Dear Reggie,
>
> Thanks for the great experience. I hope this will look good in your trophy room, where it can be enjoyed by you and your guests. Beth and I had a wonderful time. Keep up the good work.
>
> Sincerely,
> Harry

"This will look good in the trophy room," Reggie exclaimed. "He was so excited about bagging this lion; I can't believe he could live without it."

Chapter Twenty-two

Harry's headaches became more frequent and more severe. At first, he'd been able to get rid of them with aspirin, but now it provided little relief. He knew the time was growing short.

He and Beth were doing OK. He'd decided not to ask her to marry him. It wouldn't be fair. She seemed preoccupied lately, too, as if she had a lot on her mind. He worried that maybe she was drinking too much, despite not having seen her drinking at all, but she looked a little rough in the morning. Harry was relieved that she had things in her life to keep her busy while he was completing the final missions in his life. They went to movies and for walks in the park. They fed the squirrels from a bench, and spent as much quality time as they could. When they were together, it was as if nothing was wrong. It was like magic. Harry wished that he'd met Beth sooner, so they would have had more time, but that was not to be. His condition was progressing rapidly and the end was near. He decided that when the headaches were unbearable and confusion began to consume him, he would do the hardest thing he'd ever had to do in his life. He would send her away. The time was rapidly approaching.

Beth was worried about Harry. She watched as he struggled with headaches. He tried to hide them from her, but she noticed the amount of aspirin he took and the prescription medications. She hoped he would tell her what was wrong when he was ready, but she worried. They took their time together seriously. He was so attentive to her needs that she could almost believe everything was OK, but she knew it wasn't. He wasn't the same as he was before their vacation. There was an air of peace about him she hadn't seen before. She didn't know what to make of it. It was obvious that he still loved her and cherished every moment they shared together. Beth had to talk to him about something important, something that wouldn't wait, but this was not the time.

Chapter Twenty-three

Leo sat in the waiting room of the United States Disciplinary Barracks at Fort Leavenworth, waiting for a prisoner to be brought in for an interview. He'd been here many times before. He was a chaser in the Marines and had to bring prisoners to and from the prison many times. He was accustomed to the atmosphere.

Prisoner 63821 was brought in and sat in front of Leo behind bulletproof glass.

Leo stared at him for a moment. He wanted to let him stew and put him on the defensive. After a few moments, he queried, "Terrance Prevatt?"

"Who the hell are you?" the prisoner asked.

"Name's Leo."

"What do you want, Leo?" the smug criminal asked.

"I want you to tell me about William Holt," Leo said, as he leaned back in his chair.

Prevatt was surprised. He didn't expect to hear that name ever again; it had been a decade. He felt his stomach tighten and his hands sweat. "I don't know any William Holt," he replied.

"Bullshit! I can tell by the look on your face you know exactly who I'm talking about."

"What if I do? That shit was years ago."

"I don't care about you, asshole. I'm here about William. He's serving a life sentence for you."

"He got seven years, and he was out in five."

"So you've been following what happened. Obviously, you do care."

Prevatt, a former officer now convicted of another crime and serving a seven-year sentence of his own, felt a bit of remorse for what he'd done to Bill. He was just a scapegoat for Prevatt's greed. He looked down at the handcuffs on his wrists and said, "What could I do? I was a young officer. I didn't want to go to prison. I had a way out, and I took it. I'm sorry for what it did to him, but what happened, happened. I can't change that now."

"You can change it for Bill. You can stand up and take responsibility for what you did. You can clear his name."

"And put a fresh sentence on top of the one I have now? I don't think so," Prevatt said, leaning back in his seat.

Leo leaned forward, stared the convict right in the eyes, and said, "What if I could guarantee it wouldn't cost you a single extra day in here?"

The smug man looked up at Leo, and their eyes met.

Leo saw a glimmer of hope and continued. "What do you think life is going to be like when you get out of here? You think you are going to be able to find a job? What if I told you that when you got out, there would be something waiting for you out there that would make civilian life easier?"

Leo had his attention now. He was talking about money, and money was what this guy was all about.

"You don't come clean and clear Holt's name and I will be there to make sure that you are on the street," Leo continued. "The choice is yours, help yourself, or have me on your case for the rest of my career."

"What do you want me to do?"

Leo reached in his jacket and pulled out a notepad and a pen. "Start from the beginning."

Chapter Twenty-four

Harry was on his way home. The symptoms were getting out of control. His hands were shaky, his speech was changing, and his headaches were getting worse. Soon it would be impossible to hide his condition from Beth. It was time to do the thing that he dreaded more than dying; it was time to send Beth away.

He wanted to make love to her one more time, but didn't think that was right, or fair. His dread of the imminent conversation was worse than his fear of death, but it had to be done. He couldn't let her watch him decay and die. That would be even worse.

Beth was waiting for Harry to get home. They needed to talk. She'd been waiting for the right time, when he wasn't so preoccupied and could listen to her, but matters had to be discussed that could no longer wait.

Harry walked into the apartment. She began to rush over to him, but was stopped short by the awful look on his face. She asked, "Are you all right?"

"I need you to do something for me," he responded.

"You know I'd do anything for you, baby," she replied. She thought she was about to learn what had been bothering him all this time.

"I need you to go stay with your parents for a while," he said coldly.

Beth was dumbfounded. "With my parents? Why?

"I don't want to get into that, baby, but you'll understand later."

"I want to be with you. Did I do something wrong?" she asked.

"No, my love, but there's something that I have to do, and I can't do it with you here. I love you with all my heart and would love for you to stay, but you can't be here, not right now. I'll send for you when it's time for you to come back, and then you'll understand why it was so important for you to leave."

She took the last few steps toward him, wrapped her arms around him, and pulled him tight. "I don't want to go away," she said, tears rolling down her face "I want to stay here with you."

"I want that too, baby, but it can't be." He was crying, too. "Do you trust me?"

"Of course I do," she said through her tears.

"Then trust me that this is the right thing to do," he said. "I'll send someone to bring you back when it's time. Until then, don't ask any questions, please. Just go."

"How long?" she asked.

"Not long, but be ready when I send for you."

"I will," she said. "When do I have to go?"

"Right now, tonight," he said as he handed her an envelope. "This should tide you over until I send for you. Don't cry, baby. This is for the best. Trust me."

"I do trust you," she said. "Will I see you again?" she asked.

"Yes, when I send for you."

She looked up at him and pressed her face close to his. He kissed her passionately and almost asked her to stay, but he didn't. He knew this was for the best.

He turned and, without another word, walked out of the apartment and into the elevator. He turned to face her, staring into her eyes as the doors slid closed.

The apartment was silent. She didn't get a chance to tell him what was on her mind; it would have to wait again. She didn't know how long, but she hoped he would call her home soon. She didn't know what was going on. She really didn't know much about what he did for a living. Could he be in trouble?

But she trusted him and would do as he asked, even though it was killing her. She went into the bedroom, packed her bags, and said goodbye to the apartment for what she hoped was only a short time. She went down the elevator and off into the world, a world she hadn't been in for a long while…without Harry.

Harry watched from the shadows as she left the building and hailed a cab. She was so beautiful and he loved her so much. It was all so unfair. He cursed his life, his luck, and this heartless disease that was torturing him in every way. Not only was it going to kill him, it was going to keep him from the best thing that ever happened to him. It was going to keep him from Beth.

He went upstairs when he was sure that she was gone. He couldn't eat. The end was getting close; he could feel it. But there were still things to do. He had to get ready for Beth's return.

Chapter Twenty-five

Bill Holt sat in the military courtroom as Terrence Prevatt told the story of how he had framed Bill, who was innocent of all charges. The prosecutor made a deal to allow his time for the crime against Bill to be served concurrently with the time he was already serving. The judge didn't like it, but at least a wrong was being corrected. At the end of the hearing, Bill was ordered to stand.

"It is the finding of this court that a great injustice has been done to a fine officer with an otherwise impeccable record. Furthermore, it is the order of this court that William Holt's record be expunged of this incident, and the rank of captain be reinstated along with time in grade and back pay from the time of his wrongful conviction. It is also ordered that his dishonorable discharge be immediately changed to an honorable discharge with the apology of this court."

With that, Captain William Holt spoke up. "Your Honor, if it pleases the court, I would rather rejoin my unit."

The judge smiled. "Very well, it is so ordered. Captain Holt will be reinstated in the Marine Corps and reassigned to Second Force Recon Battalion." The gavel dropped and the judge said, "Welcome back, son."

As the judge stood to leave the courtroom, the bailiff stood and said, "All rise!"

Harry stood in the gallery with Leo, and then shook hands with Bill as the courtroom cleared.

"How can I ever thank you, Harry?" Bill asked, clutching his hand.

"Be a good Marine," he said.

"I will, sir. You can count on it."

****

Harry sat in Dr. Young's office as he'd done before, sipping coffee and trying to relax. Everything except the couch, a chair, and the coffee table were gone. The place was empty from attic to basement. Grace sat in her chair with a scarf tied around her head and sunglasses protecting her eyes from the light coming in the now-bare windows.

"Well, Harry, have you made good use of your time?" she asked.

"I think so," he replied. "At least I've tried to."

"So what's next for you?"

"I don't know. I miss Beth so badly, but I don't want her to watch me suffer. I've accomplished the things I wanted to do for the people I wanted to help. I think I just need some diversion."

"Good, Harry. Now it's time to accept what's going to happen. Take it all in while you can. I know I will."

Harry paused for a second…then it came to him; the empty office, her deep understanding of his condition, and what he was going through. She was dying as well. He acted as if he'd known all along. "I guess this is our last visit."

"Yes, Harry. I'd like to continue to see you, but I'm leaving for Africa," she said as she removed her scarf and wig, showing him her baldness from her chemotherapy treatments. "I spent some time there with the Peace Corps many years ago and have been back many times over the years. I'd like to go back again while I still can."

"Sounds like a plan," Harry said as he sipped his coffee. "I wish I could go with you."

They looked at each other for a moment and smiled.

"You could if you wanted to, Harry, but it's a primitive life. The people I'm going to live with are a simple tribe living on a small river. There is no running water, no electricity, and no phones."

"Sounds like just what I need," he said.

"Are you sure?" Grace asked.

"When do we leave?" Harry said with commitment.

Harry had, finally, become a carefree man. Since he'd completed all the things he wanted to do, his headaches seemed to abate somewhat. He'd done all he could for others. This sounded like an adventure that he'd now like to try. Besides, what could it hurt? He was going to die. He wanted to be in his bed for that, but until then, he was going to go with the flow.

****

The journey to the village was a complex one. From the commercial airport, they had to take a bush plane to a remote airstrip and finally a dugout canoe to the village.

They were met by the tribe who knew Grace from the visits she'd made over the many years. She'd helped teach the children English and brought supplies. She'd enjoyed her time there, and they welcomed her with open arms but looked a little distrustfully at Harry. After Grace talked to them, they cautiously accepted him as well.

If it had not been for his previous excursion into the Dark Continent, Harry would have been completely out of his element. He felt as though he was missing something. It was Beth. He was really yearned for her. He wished he could hang on longer. But he was showing signs and struggling with pain most of the time. He wondered if maybe he sent her away too soon on his better days. However, he would have a bad day where he would lose time and get angry for no reason, and he knew he had made the right decision. It was those days when he needed Grace to take care of him. She knew just what to do and how to deal with him. Those days were few and far between, but they were getting closer together and more pronounced as time went on.

Grace and Harry became very close, like brother and sister. They worked with the tribe together, and they lived in the same accommodations. The two stayed in a hut built over the river's edge. The sunsets were beautiful, the air was clear, the food was terrible, and the mosquitoes were vicious, but here, far away from his world, he found the peace he'd been looking for.

Nothing here was familiar to him. The entire world of dreams that drove him was absent, and somehow, it assuaged his feelings of loss. In the evenings, they gathered and shared food from the river or whatever the hunters of the tribe could harvest. After dinner, they sat around the fire and told stories about past hunts or ancestors or the stars. There were no board meetings, no production schedules, and no talk of who was trying to steal whose job. There was no bitterness, no busy intersections, and no freeloaders.

The tribe lived in harmony. Everyone pitched in for the common good, and Harry did his part. In the beginning, he was able to hunt with the men, and he loved it. It wasn't like the hunt in Kenya; here, they hunted with spears and cunning. They hunted as a team, each doing his job. They surrounded and drove the hunted to the hunters. It didn't matter which one made the kill. They weren't concerned with trying to win a trophy. They were trying to feed the tribe. There was no envy, no jealousy, no bickering, and no squabbling. They did what had to be done. They had what they needed, and they had each other.

Harry watched Grace blend with the tribe. She was one of them. She didn't have to try to gain acceptance; she already had it. Grace worked and laughed with them and let the world fall away. The concerns of the civilized world didn't exist here. It was strange, but it didn't matter that they were dying. Here, dying was a part of life. It wasn't important if one person survived; it was only important that the tribe survive.

Harry soon found himself in the same world as Grace. In the months he lived with them, he quit worrying about his own identity and just thought about the tribe. In the beginning, when the hunters went out on a hunt, if he could catch them, they allowed him to go. If not, they left him behind, but after a while, the tribe called to him before they left. And, finally, they would wait for him, as if it were his duty to be with them.

On his last hunt with the tribe, he was the hunter who made the kill. The beaters had driven unknown game through high grass. Suddenly, a warthog sprang out of the cover directly in front of Harry. One of the hunters threw a net over the beast, and Harry drove his spear deep into it, over and over, until it was dead. It was primal, it was violent, but in a sense, it was natural. And unlike the hunt for the kudu, it was necessary. Even killing the lion to save Beth wasn't necessary. They hadn't had to be there in the first place. This kill was to feed a tribe.

Afterwards, around the campfire, as the hunters told the story of the hunt, he heard his name among the words, some of which were English, but mostly of the native tongue. The storyteller acted out the hunt as he led the tribe through the details verbally. And when it came to Harry's kill, he pointed to Harry and, holding a spear, simulated Harry's attack on the beast. He'd never felt more like one of them. The rest of the tribe shouted with excitement as the storyteller imitated Harry spearing the warthog over and over again. Finally, they looked at him as one of their own.

As time went on, Harry found himself getting too weak to hunt, but he remembered watching the guides from his hunt in Kenya, so he helped butcher the game. He fished in the river with nets that the women of the tribe made, and one night, the tribe turned to Harry, waiting for him to tell the story around the campfire. It was an honor; it meant that the tribe fully accepted him as one of their own. And there was only one story that he could tell that they would understand, the story of a herd of kudu, a killer lion, and a quick shot that saved the love of his life. They listened intently as he told of his adventure, and those who could speak English translated for those who didn't. Everyone, young and old, enjoyed the story, and when it was done they presented him with his own spear, handmade by the tribe, signifying they considered him a mighty hunter. He admired the spear and the detail that the tribe put into it. Carvings on the shaft told the story of Harry coming to the tribe, his blending with the tribe, hunting with them, and finally Harry killing the warthog. He found himself loving it more than any of his possessions. Even more than the Mercedes that was a symbol of having arrived.

One morning, Grace awoke to find Harry wasn't in his hammock. Worried, she went to look for him. She didn't have to look far. He was swimming in the river just outside the hut. She watched as the gentle current carried him past the window. He had a look of peace on his noticeably thinning face. He floated on his back with his face just above the surface.

"Having fun?" she asked as she came down the steps to the shoreline.

"Yep," Harry responded. "Join me?"

"Don't mind if I do." She slid into the warm water.

"It's time for me to go home."

"Is it?" Grace asked.

"It's getting close now, I can feel it," Harry admitted.

She didn't want to mention it, but she'd noticed he wasn't eating, had lost a lot of weight, and didn't look good. His eyes were sunken and he was moving more slowly.

"Will you go with me?" he asked.

"You want me to?" she returned.

"Please. I'm scared. I mean you're like a sister to me. I need your support. I have one more thing to do."

"What's that?"

"I want to see Beth one more time."

After a short pause, she replied, "I'll go with you."

"Thank you, Grace," he said. "You've been a great friend. I know you're taking your own advice and making a difference for the tribe, but I appreciate you doing this for me."

"You don't understand, Harry," she said. "You are my cause. My treasure of time is what I spend with you."

Chapter Twenty-six

Beth awoke to loud knocking on the front door of her parent's house. "Was this it?" she wondered. Once at the door, she found a large, well-dressed man she'd never seen before.

"Who is it?" she asked through the closed door.

"My name is Leo. I'm looking for Beth."

She opened the door. "I'm Beth."

"Harry sent me to bring you home."

"Please, come in," she said. "How is he?"

"He needs to see you," he replied. "How soon can you leave?"

"Let me throw some things in a bag and say goodbye to my parents," she said as she headed for the bedroom.

"Good, we have a plane to catch," Leo said, checking his watch.

She hurried to pack and say her goodbyes. Leo took her bags and escorted her to a rental car. He helped her in, threw the bags in the trunk, and they were off. Beth could hardly contain herself. In the last few months, she'd almost given up hope. She'd tried to call and received no answer. His office said he'd taken a leave of absence. He didn't answer his cell phone. She was sure he loved her and he'd said he would send for her. Her father said he was a bum, that he'd ruined her life and moved on to some other unsuspecting girl. Her mother said, if he was avoiding her, he would probably never call again.

"What did they know," she thought. Here was Leo sent to bring her back, just as Harry said.

Now they could get married and be a family. All her dreams would come true.

Leo, seeing the condition that she was in, focused on keeping her in the dark as Harry had told him to do. It almost brought tears to his eyes, knowing what was about to happen, but he was a professional and would keep his emotions in check.

Beth tried to pry information out of Leo, but he played dumb. He kept saying the same thing: "All I know is that I was sent to bring you back as soon as possible. I'm sorry."

They sat together in the airport terminal, waiting for their flight. It was grueling, waiting for something out of her control. She tried to get her mind off of it by thinking of when she met Harry and how he changed her life. It had been hard to leave him. It was even harder to return, but she did as he asked. She'd pined for him every day, running to the phone each time it rang, hoping it was him. Other than a couple of letters Harry sent, telling her how much he missed her and repeating he would send for her when it was time, she had no contact. Thank God all this was about to be over.

It was a short plane ride, but, to Beth, it seemed like days. She followed Leo down the jetway, picked up her luggage, and they were on their way. They arrived at the apartment's parking garage and she hurried to the elevator. Leo had the key that allowed them to go to the penthouse. He inserted the key and the door closed. Beth could hardly contain herself. She didn't know why she was sent away, and she didn't care. She was home now. She was going to be with him again. She would love him and make him glad she was home.

She watched as the lights in the elevator flicked from one floor to the next, slowly, as though there was nothing more important than their little job of showing what floor they were on. The doors finally slid open, and she rushed into the apartment. She didn't notice anything different; her eyes were busy looking for Harry. He wasn't in the living room or on the balcony, so she raced to the bedroom. There she found an unknown woman standing between her and the bedroom. She stopped Beth before she entered and introduced herself.

"Hi, you must be Beth. My name is Dr. Grace Young. It's good to meet you at last," she said, holding out her hand.

Beth half-heartedly took her hand and stared in confusion at the woman who looked more like a patient than a doctor. "Where is Harry?" she asked.

Then she heard a dry, weak voice that she hardly recognized in the bedroom. "I'm here, baby."

The voice came from the bed. She walked over and couldn't believe her eyes. There lay Harry, or rather the shell of what Harry had been. He held out his hand to her. He looked so thin, like malnutrition and disease had taken their toll. His eyes were sunken, and his hands and arms were bony. She'd only been away for a few months, and he looked like a different person, like an old, sick man. Tears rolled down her face.

"Oh, my God, Harry," she cried out. "What's going on?"

"Now you see why you had to go, my love," he said. "I couldn't bear for you to watch me go through these last few months, but I had to see you again. I had to tell you one more time how much I love you. I had to look into your eyes and see your love for me. I had to smell your hair and feel your touch once more before I go. I was afraid you wouldn't get here in time."

Beth turned in desperation to Dr. Young. "Isn't there anything that can be done? Can't we save him?"

"I'm sorry, Beth. There's nothing to be done but manage his pain."

Beth turned back to him. He stared at her, and through his love and tears, he managed, "It'll be OK, baby. I'll always be with you."

Beth took his hand and placed it on her swollen belly, "Yes, you will," she said. "This is what I wanted to tell you before you sent me away."

Harry smiled as he moved his hand over her belly. "I'm gonna be a daddy?" he asked. He turned to Grace. "You hear that, Grace? I'm gonna be a dad!"

Grace had taken his other hand, and they smiled together. "I heard, Harry. Congratulations."

Then she put his hand down and said, "I'll leave you two alone now," and quietly left the room.

Beth climbed into the bed and put her head on his shoulder the way she had so many times before. She snuggled up to him with his hand on her stomach, and he kissed the top of her head. They talked and shared and made the most of the moments they could pry away from death.

They lay there together for a long while, and then, very quietly, Harry slipped away.

Beth felt him go and held him tightly as long as she could. Then she got out of the bed and went to get Grace. "He's gone," she said, tears flowing again.

Grace, who'd been sitting in the living room with Leo, walked into the bedroom and closed the door. Leo walked over to Beth and let her cry on his shoulder. "Let's get out of here and get some air," he said.

They entered the elevator and went down to the lobby as Grace called to make the funeral arrangements, the last task she had promised to do for her new brother.

"I'm sorry I couldn't tell you. Harry didn't want you to know. He didn't want you to suffer any more than necessary," Leo told Beth.

"I understand, but I wish he'd let me stay with him. Why did he send me away?" she asked.

"Harry had a rough time. He knew it was going to be bad, and he didn't want you to remember him that way. You can see how quickly he went downhill. He didn't want you to take that ride with him. Remember him the way he was before."

She buried her face in Leo's burly chest, crying uncontrollably. He held her tightly. Leo was a stranger, but she'd spent more time with him than with Grace, and she needed someone strong to hold her. All her hopes and dreams were gone, and she felt so alone.

Chapter Twenty-seven

The funeral was uneventful. There were people Harry had worked with, his brother Charlie, and several cousins and nephews. A Marine officer in his class “A” service uniform sat in the back of the church, alone. He looked completely out of place. Leo seemed to be the only person who knew him. Grace was there, and Stan Jacobson and Steve Simmons. They talked quietly to each other. Each person visited Harry’s casket in turn to say goodbye.

Beth, dressed in black, cried quietly as she looked at Harry. She reached out to hold his hand, the hand that was once so powerful, yet touched her so tenderly, now cold and frail. It looked like the hand of an old man. His face, once chiseled and strong, which looked at her with such love and affection, was now unfamiliar to her. She bent down, kissed him gently one last time, and took her seat. The service was respectful, and Harry was laid to rest. The finality of it was unstoppable. Harry was no more.

Beth went back to the apartment and tried to decide what to do. In his will, Harry had left everything to her. She would not have to worry about money again, for her or her unborn child. She looked at the apartment in a new light. It was hers now, although it would never be the same without Harry. It was then that she noticed the changes. A marlin hung on the wall in the living room. The paintings Harry loved so much were gone, and in their place were enlargements of pictures—the photos of Beth he’d taken with the camera she bought him. There were pictures of them on the beach together at Conception Island, of him in the fighting chair on *Dividends* as he fought the marlin, of them on the wreck dive before his mishap with the goliath grouper, and the one Reggie had taken of them kneeling over the dead lion that had tried to make a meal of her. She looked at each one and studied every pixel, reliving the experiences again and again. Little trinkets they'd purchased each other along the way were placed with care around the apartment. On the mantle was the conch shell she'd given him after their first dive together. It was mounted on a plaque as if it were a prized trophy.

Then, on the bar, she saw it. It wasn't there before when she walked past the bar, she was sure of it. But there it was all the same. It was a little, felt-covered box with a domed top, the same box she'd seen in the drawer at the hunting lodge. She picked it up and thought about opening it. Then she noticed the letter beneath it. She opened that instead and read the contents.

> My Dearest Beth,
>
> If you are reading this, I am gone. I'm sorry I had to send you away. I hope you can understand my decision. I loved you too much to put you through what I was about to go through.
>
> I had always intended to ask you to marry me. In this little box is the ring I bought you in the Cayman Islands. I was waiting for the right time. I guess I waited too long.
>
> I wish I would've met you sooner. I would've loved to have children with you. We would have been great parents together. But, I guess it was not to be.
>
> I want you to remember us the way we were. Have a great life, and don't wait too long to do the things that you want to do. I did, and it cost me greatly. I'm just glad I had the chance to be with you, as it is the only part of my life that really mattered.

Live, love, and be happy. I will always be there in your heart. Someday, when your time is done, look for me, and I will be there, waiting for you. Then we can be together again.

With all my love,

Harry

She put down the letter and opened the box. There was a beautiful diamond ring inside. She could imagine Harry choosing it and giving it to her on bended knee. And, in that moment, Harry was still alive and with her. She pictured him looking up at her, asking her to be his wife. And she heard herself saying, "Yes."

Beth held on to the fantasy as long she could, but it too began to fade away. She struggled to relive it, but like the time they spent on the private beach of Conception Island, it would never be the same. She let it go.

She closed the box, refolded the letter, and stepped away from the bar. Putting her hand on her swollen belly, she said to Harry Junior, "Your father was a great man."

About the Author

J.R. Ballow was born in the hills of Kentucky to lower, middle income parents in 1963. He has three brothers and one sister, and is the youngest of all five. He moved to Clearwater, Florida, in 1974, after his father had a heart attack and was forced to retire from driving a bus.

J.R. served in the Marines in his early twenties and settled back in Florida in 1987 after his honorable discharge. He married and raised four children there. He built a successful business and ran it for fourteen years. The business consumed him, but he continued to build it until a tragedy in 2004 threw his life into a tailspin.

His eldest son took his own life at the age of thirteen, and it devastated his family. J.R. found the strength to try to live on, but he realized just how precious life is. He decided to make changes. He later was divorced from his wife, sold the business that was killing him, took flying lessons and became a pilot, started a new business, and finally sought out the love of his life, Lisa, whom he had secretly loved since high school. They were married in March 2012.

Among pilots, there is a saying: “There are things that can’t help you in the air, altitude above you, runway behind you, and distress calls that you don’t make.” J.R. believes there is another important lesson people don’t seem to realize: “There is only one thing of value in the world. It’s not money, or power, or health, or family. The only thing of real value is TIME. You can’t buy it, steal it, bargain for it, or even beg for it. All you can do is use it or waste it.”

J.R. hopes that you enjoy this book, loosely based on his own life, and that you decide to live your own lives as though each day might be the last. He hopes you will not waste “The Treasure of Time.”

www.ingramcontent.com/pod-product-compliance
Lightning Source LLC
Chambersburg PA
CBHW020327200626
46814CB00006BB/2458
9781940869452